Edmond Rostand (1868–1918) was born in Marseilles, France, the son of a distinguished and cultured family. The young Rostand was educated first in Marseilles, then in Paris, where he earned a degree in law. It was a profession, however, that he was never to practice. He made his literary debut in 1890 with a volume of lyric verse, and his first important play, *The Romancers*, was produced by the Comédie Française in 1894. *Cyrano de Bergerac* (1897) won critical acclaim and spectacular popular success, and Rostand further solidified his position as the foremost of modern French romantic dramatists with *L'Aiglon* (1900) and *Chantecler* (1910).

Eteel Lawson was educated in France and holds master's degrees in international relations and economics. The author of a children's book and a collection of short stories, she worked for the United Nations in Paris and now lives on the French Riviera.

Professor of French and Francophone Studies at Vassar College, **Cynthia B. Kerr** earned a Ph.D. in French and Humanities from Stanford University. Specializing in performance studies and Early Modern France, she has published three books, including *Corneille à l'affiche: vingt ans de créations théâtrales, 1980–2000*. She is the author of more than eighty articles and book reviews published in journals in Europe and the United States. She regularly writes for *Choice*, the publication of the American Library Association.

Cyrano de Bergerac

A Heroic Comedy in Five Acts

Edmond Rostand

TRANSLATED BY LOWELL BAIR

WITH AN INTRODUCTION BY ETEEL LAWSON

AND A NEW AFTERWORD BY CYNTHIA B. KERR

SIGNET CLASSICS

SIGNET CLASSICS
Published by New American Library, a division of
Penguin Group (USA) Inc., 375 Hudson Street,
New York, New York 10014, USA
Penguin Group (Canada), 90 Eglinton Avenue East, Suite 700, Toronto,
Ontario M4P 2Y3, Canada (a division of Pearson Penguin Canada Inc.)
Penguin Books Ltd., 80 Strand, London WC2R 0RL, England
Penguin Ireland, 25 St. Stephen's Green, Dublin 2,
Ireland (a division of Penguin Books Ltd.)
Penguin Group (Australia), 250 Camberwell Road, Camberwell, Victoria 3124,
Australia (a division of Pearson Australia Group Pty. Ltd.)
Penguin Books India Pvt. Ltd., 11 Community Centre, Panchsheel Park,
New Delhi - 110 017, India
Penguin Group (NZ), 67 Apollo Drive, Rosedale, Auckland 0632,
New Zealand (a division of Pearson New Zealand Ltd.)
Penguin Books (South Africa) (Pty.) Ltd., 24 Sturdee Avenue,
Rosebank, Johannesburg 2196, South Africa

Penguin Books Ltd., Registered Offices:
80 Strand, London WC2R 0RL, England

Published by Signet Classics, an imprint of New American Library,
a division of Penguin Group (USA) Inc.

First Signet Classics Printing, May 1972
First Signet Classics Printing (Kerr Afterword), March 2012
20 19 18 17 16 15 14

Translation copyright © Lowell Bair, 1972
Introduction copyright © Eteel Lawson, 2003
Afterword copyright © Cynthia B. Kerr, 2012
All rights reserved

Ⓒ REGISTERED TRADEMARK—MARCA REGISTRADA

Printed in the United States of America

It was to Cyrano's soul that I intended
to dedicate this poem.
But since his soul has passed into you,
Coquelin,* I dedicate it to you.

—E. R.

* Benoît-Constant Coquelin (1841–1909) was the French actor
who played the part of Cyrano when the play opened in 1897. (All
footnotes are by the translator.)

Contents

Introduction

December 28, 1897. Minutes before the curtain rose on the opening night of *Cyrano de Bergerac,* Edmond Rostand faced his lead actor, Constant Coquelin, and said, "I beg your forgiveness, my friend. Pardon me for having involved you in a disastrous adventure."* Not even the playwright himself believed that the play would see the phenomenal success that immediately followed. At a time when the European stage was dominated by realism, audiences were accustomed to unsentimental depictions of the grim, harsh realities of society. In France in particular, this movement developed into naturalism, which vested in theater the additional task of explaining the scientific laws of human nature. But unlike the works of Gustave Flaubert and Émile Zola, which set the tone for the time by addressing social ills such as poverty, sickness, and crime, Rostand's *Cyrano de Bergerac* revived the spirit of the Grand Siècle, the seventeenth century of Louis XIII and Louis XIV, with its culture of bombast, fairy tales, musketeers, and beautiful maidens. Known as the golden age, it was a time of idealism, romanticism, and military bravery, a time when great swordsmanship was as prized as—and often compared to—elaborate, eloquent verse. Much to Rostand's surprise, the play was lauded as a welcome departure and instantly secured its place among French theatrical legends. Many compared Rostand's Cyrano to d'Artag-

*Rostand, Edmond, *Cyrano de Bergerac,* Geoff Woollen, ed. p. ix. London: Bristol Classical Press, 1994.

nan, hero of *The Three Musketeers,* Alexandre Dumas's epic sentimental historical romance written more than fifty years earlier (1844); they were both gallant duelists from Gascogny ruled by chivalry, but driven by love. Among Rostand's seven plays and three volumes of poetry, none of his other works ever rivaled the success of *Cyrano de Bergerac,* which made him overnight a literary celebrity. In May 1901, at the age of thirty-three, he became the youngest member to be elected to the Académie Française. In that same year, he received the Legion of Honor, an award for cultural achievement.

Long after Rostand's death in 1918, Cyrano de Bergerac, the selfless, passionate troubadour and swashbuckling hero, remains virtually synonymous with his creator. Through Cyrano, Rostand lives on and his genius delights new generations whether they encounter this unforgettable play on the stage, on the wide screen, or in the pages of a book.

Literary works that stand the test of time touch upon universal themes, themes that move and inspire us in very similar and profound ways. *Cyrano de Bergerac* is one such play. What captured the hearts of nineteenth-century readers and spectators, and continues to capture ours now, is the depth of the story's love, passion, heroism, and moral honor. Its larger-than-life hero is extraordinary, but at the same time flawed, a combination that makes Cyrano seem quite modern and accessible. Rostand found inspiration for his romantic hero in real-life Parisian nobleman and author Savinien de Cyrano de Bergerac (1619–55). Although similarities can be found between the real Cyrano and the play's hero, Rostand freely altered and invented details to mold his own ideal. The result is a protagonist who leaps off the page and who bears every marking of a real human being. For Rostand took the conventional fairy tale hero—the charming, handsome prince embodying beauty and perfection—and made him human. This romantic hero is imperfect, disfigured, born with a face unforgiving to the human eye. Regardless of his military prowess, his great literary talent, and his unswerving honor, he considers himself hideous.

CYRANO

Oh, no, never! No, it would be grotesque if a tear ran down this nose! As long as it's in my power to prevent it, I'll never let the divine beauty of tears be sullied by such gross ugliness. There's nothing more sublime than tears, and I wouldn't want a single one of them to become an object of ridicule because of me.

(Act One, Scene V, p. 51)

It is not an army of a hundred men that is his most powerful enemy, but his nose. His battlefield is no place other than within himself. He is convinced early in life that he will never be able to conquer the one thing dear to him—love. To Cyrano, his unworthiness is literally as plain as the nose on his face. If he cannot get past his outer imperfection to see his inner beauty, how could anyone else? To his friends, he seems a heroic giant, but he shrinks from love underneath a tortured soul.

CYRANO

. . . this nose of mine, which precedes me by a quarter of an hour wherever I go, forbids me ever to dream of being loved by even an ugly woman.

(Act One, Scene V, p. 49)

His wit, talent, and heroism are no match for his physical shortcomings. His ugliness defines him and overshadows his greatness.

The conflict in the play arises because, though Cyrano regards himself as the most unpleasing of men, he falls madly in love with the fairest of creatures, his cousin Roxane. Like Cyrano, Roxane breaks the mold of the romantic protagonist. As intelligent as she is beautiful, she is moved by both a handsome face and a fine intellect (with a weakness for well-turned verse). Her perfection mirrors and mocks Cyrano's imperfection. He suffers in silence, for he feels not just sure of her rejection but deserving of it. He is no Romeo to this Juliet, as he reminds his confidant, Le Bret, who tries to cheer him up.

CYRANO

No! I love Cleopatra—do I look like a Caesar? I adore Berenice—have I the appearance of a Titus?

(Act One, Scene V, p. 51)

Of course, it is inner beauty that Cyrano represents, and as Act One proceeds, Rostand shifts his emphasis from Cyrano's outer appearance to the content of his character. In these scenes, Rostand presents a man who excels at everything. Cyrano is a natural leader, courageous soldier, brilliant swordsman, scientist, musician—and most of all, an uncanny master of language, exemplified by his famous monologue about his nose (Act One, Scene IV, pp. 38–39) and the poem he composes while fighting a duel (Act One, Scene IV, p. 43). Readers lose sight of the nose amid the countless displays of his intelligence, heroism, and talent. The sharp contrast between his aesthetic shortcomings and the greatness of his soul is powerful and effective.

Cyrano's antithesis is Christian, a cadet in Cyrano's company. He is a brave and noble soldier who has looks, but not brains. He is the simplest of blokes, but his beauty equals Roxane's. He too finds himself in love with her and fears that his dull wit will prevent him from having her. At the turning point of the play, Cyrano decides to seize the chance to express his feelings for Roxane—to love fully, even if never to be loved—and promises to help Christian woo Roxane. By combining their powers—beauty and wit—the two men will become one.

CHRISTIAN

Ah, if only I could express myself gracefully!

CYRANO

If only I had a handsome face!

* * *

CHRISTIAN

I need eloquence, and I have none!

CYRANO

I'll lend you mine! Lend me your conquering physical charm, and together we'll form a romantic hero!

* * *

CYRANO

. . . Shall we complete each other? We'll walk together: you in the light, I in the shadows. I'll make you eloquent, you'll make me handsome.

(Act Two, Scene X, pp. 101–102)

Together, they create an ideal, a man who does not exist. In this way, Cyrano feels he can become *whole,* but that belief is a chimera. In truth, it is deceptive and cowardly, and Cyrano's honor is somewhat tarnished. But who can remain unsympathetic to Cyrano's desire to express his passion from behind a borrowed mask of beauty and, vice versa, for Christian to use another's eloquent words to win the heart of his beloved? The fulfillment of their desires carries more weight with them than maintaining their integrity, and both men lie to the woman who is the object of their affections.

The power of this duo is manifest in some of the most famous scenes of the play. Like Juliet, Roxane stands on her balcony as Christian woos her from below. His attempts without Cyrano's aid are weak: "I love you," "I adore you." Roxane is terribly disappointed with his vanished eloquence; it's almost as if he becomes *ugly* to her. Then Cyrano comes to the rescue, first feeding lines to Christian and ultimately speaking them himself. Hidden by the veil of darkness, Cyrano can at last freely express the love he has in his heart. The effect on him is dizzying, almost disorienting, as he reveals himself by speaking his true feelings. Roxane remarks on the change in him:

ROXANE

Perhaps it's true—even your voice is different.

CYRANO

Yes, quite different, because in the protecting darkness, I dare at last be myself, I dare . . . What was I saying? I don't know. . . . All this . . . Excuse my agitation! All this is so enchanting . . . so new to me.

(Act Three, Scene VII, p. 127)

The deceit works like a charm; Cyrano's poetic phrases have her hopelessly in love with Christian, unaware that it is Cyrano's soul that she adores.

ROXANE

Yes, I'm trembling, and I'm weeping, and I love you, and I'm yours! You've made me drunk with love! (Act Three, Scene VII, p. 130)

By the end of Act Three, Christian and Roxane are husband and wife.

Act Four opens on a scene of war. The French are beseiging Arras, one of the key battles in the Thirty Years' War (1618–48). The mood of the play shifts from comic to serious. The romantic hero, the ideal man who neither Christian nor Cyrano could be, shatters.

Roxane risks her own life to reach her husband by passing through the Spanish lines, compelled by the overwhelming beauty of Christian's letters. Of course, it is Cyrano who wrote the letters—and risked his own life by crossing enemy lines twice a day to send them to Roxane.

Roxane has come to ask her husband for forgiveness; she admits having loved him at first for the beauty of his face, then for a combination of his appearance and his soul. Now, however, she cherishes him exclusively for his soul, as revealed in his letters. The news saddens Christian, for it means Roxane cannot be in love with him at all, but with Cyrano's poetic soul.

CHRISTIAN

I don't want it! I want to be loved simply for . . .

ROXANE

For what women have always loved in you till now? Let me love you in a better way!

CHRISTIAN

No! It was better before!

ROXANE

You don't know what you are saying! It's better now! I didn't really love you before. It's what makes you yourself that I now love. If you were less handsome . . .

CHRISTIAN

Enough!

ROXANE

I'd still love you. If you suddenly became ugly . . .

CHRISTIAN

Oh, don't say that!

ROXANE

I *will* say it!

CHRISTIAN

Even if I were ugly? . . .

ROXANE

Yes, even if you were ugly! I swear I'd still love
you!   (Act Four, Scene VIII, p. 186)

And so a chance opens before Cyrano. Christian urges
him to confess their scheme so that Roxane might
choose between them. But still incapable of believing
that he could ever be loved, Cyrano hesitates—and the
chance is lost. Christian is mortally wounded, and Cyrano's chivalry demands he tell Christian a comforting lie:
Roxane knows the truth and still chooses him. Likewise,
he refuses to tarnish his friend's memory or make a
mockery out of Roxane's mourning. He will never reveal
the real soul behind Christian's letters. He renounces his
chance at being loved.

The final act of the play is a testament to how far
Cyrano will rise in the ranks of self-sacrifice and courage. Fifteen years have gone by and Cyrano visits Roxane every Saturday in the convent where she has found
refuge since her husband's death. Many things have
changed for these two characters. Roxane lives a solitary
life among the nuns, dedicated to the memory of her
husband. Cyrano is impoverished and has made many
powerful enemies because of his unflinching principles.
But to the very end, he chooses honor above all. Even
on the verge of death, he refuses to miss his visit. As
always, he would rather die than break his word to her—
another act of self-sacrifice. And when Roxane finally
realizes it was Cyrano who wrote the letters—he whom
she has truly loved all along—he refuses to believe she
loves him. It *can't* be true, for his face has not changed.
Even with nothing and no one left to sacrifice for, he

imprisons himself in his appearance and locks up his lonely heart forever.

ROXANE
I love you! You must live!

CYRANO
No. In the fairy tale, when Beauty said, "I love you," to the prince, his ugliness melted away like snow in the warmth of the sun, but as you can see, those words have no such magic effect on me.
(Act Five, Scene VI, p. 220)

Rostand's last act has been criticized as melodramatic. But there's no denying its effectiveness in conveying powerful messages that we take with us through life: the blind importance we put on beauty and the tragedy in the self-hate that can make us feel unworthy of love and keep us from realizing our dreams. Cyrano's personality is larger than life, but his nose is even larger, for he cannot liberate himself from this outer flaw. Our hero sums up his misfortune most eloquently.

CYRANO
. . . "Philosopher, scientist, poet, swordsman, musician, aerial traveler, maker of sharp retorts, and lover (not to his advantage!) here lies Savinien de Cyrano de Bergerac, who was everything, and who was nothing." (Act Five, Scene VI, p. 222)

The power of this eternal hero is magical. He is adored by millions around the world, and he leaves an indelible mark on our hearts. Cyrano's life is a reminder of the limitations we inflict on ourselves. If there is one lesson to be learned from the timeless, grandiloquent Cyrano de Bergerac, it is that we are truly our own worst enemy.

—Eteel Lawson

Cyrano de
Bergerac

Dramatis Personae

Cyrano de Bergerac
Christian de Neuvillette
Count de Guiche
Ragueneau
Le Bret
Carbon de Castel-Jaloux
The Cadets
Lignière
Viscount de Valvert
A Marquis
Second Marquis
Third Marquis
Montfleury
Bellerose
Jodelet
Cuigy
D'Artagnan
Brissaille
A Meddler
A Musketeer
Second Musketeer
A Spanish Officer
A Light-Horseman
The Doorkeeper
A Burgher
A Thief
A Spectator
A Guardsman
Bertrandou the Fifer
The Capuchin

Two Musicians
Poets
Pastry Cooks

Roxane
Sister Marthe
Lise
The Refreshment Girl
Mother Marguerite de Jésus
The Duenna
Sister Claire
An Actress
The Soubrette
Pages
The Flower Girl
A Lady
A Lady Intellectual
A Nun

Crowd, Burghers, Marquis, Musketeers, Thieves, Pastry Cooks, Poets, Cadets, Gascons, Actors, Violinists, Pages, Children, Spanish Soldiers, Spectators, Lady Intellectuals, Actresses, Nuns, etc.

The first four acts are set in 1640, the fifth in 1655.

Act One

⟡

A Performance at the Hôtel de Bourgogne*

The auditorium of the Hôtel de Bourgogne in 1640.

It resembles an indoor tennis court, decorated and fitted out for theatrical performances.

It is a long rectangle, seen diagonally, so that one side forms the background, extending from downstage right to upstage left, where it forms an angle with the stage, which is seen obliquely.

There are benches on both sides of this stage. The curtain consists of two tapestries that can be drawn apart. Above the proscenium, the royal arms. Broad steps from the stage to the floor of the auditorium. Places for musicians on both sides of these steps. A row of candles for footlights.

The top section of the gallery on one side is divided into boxes. No seats in the front of the audito-

---

* A theater whose full name was the Théâtre de l'Hôtel de Bourgogne, the word *hôtel* being used here with its old meaning of "mansion" or "town house." The Hôtel de Bourgogne was the Paris residence of the Dukes of Burgundy (Bourgogne) in the fourteenth and fifteenth centuries. In 1548, when it had been partially demolished, a theater was built on its site and named after the original building.

rium, whose floor is the stage of the actual theater. At the back—that is, downstage right—are benches arranged in tiers. A staircase leads to the upper seats; only its lower part is visible. Under it is a refreshment table adorned with little candelabra, vases of flowers, crystal goblets, plates of pastry, bottles, etc.

Upstage center, under the boxes, is the entrance to the auditorium, a big double door partially opened to admit the audience. On the panels of this door, as well as in several corners and above the refreshment table, are red posters bearing the name of the play: La Clorise.

As the curtain rises, the auditorium is in semidarkness, and still empty. The chandeliers have been lowered to the middle of the floor and are waiting to be lighted.

Scene I

The Audience, arriving little by little. Cavaliers, Burghers, Lackeys, Pages, Thieves, the Doorkeeper, etc., then the Marquis, Cuigy, Brissaille, the Refreshment Girl, the Volinists, etc.

(A tumult of voices is heard from outside the door, then a CAVALIER *enters abruptly.)*

THE DOORKEEPER
(Pursuing him)
Stop! You haven't paid your fifteen sols!

THE CAVALIER
I don't have to pay!

THE DOORKEEPER
Why not?

THE CAVALIER
I'm a light-horseman of the King's Household.

THE DOORKEEPER
(To another CAVALIER *who has just entered)*
And you?

SECOND CAVALIER

I don't have to pay either.

THE DOORKEEPER

But . . .

SECOND CAVALIER

I'm a musketeer.

FIRST CAVALIER
(To the second)
The play doesn't begin till two o'clock and the floor is empty. Let's have a little fencing practice.
(They fence with the foils they have brought.)

A LACKEY
(Entering)
Psst! . . . Flanquin! . . .

SECOND LACKEY
(Who has already arrived)
Yes, Champagne?

FIRST LACKEY
(Showing him what he takes out of his doublet)
Look: I have cards and dice. *(Sits down on the floor.)* Let's play.

SECOND LACKEY
(Also sitting down)
Good idea, my friend.

FIRST LACKEY
(Takes a candle stub from his pocket, lights it, and sets it on the floor.)
I've stolen a little light from my master.

A GUARDSMAN
(To a FLOWER GIRL coming toward him)
It's nice of you to come before the lights are lit!
(Takes hold of her waist.)

ONE OF THE FENCERS
(Receiving a thrust of his opponent's foil)
Touché!

ONE OF THE CARD PLAYERS

A club!

THE GUARDSMAN
(Pursuing the FLOWER GIRL*)*
A kiss!

THE FLOWER GIRL
(Pushing him away)
They'll see us!

THE GUARDSMAN
(Pulling her into a dark corner)
No danger of that!

A MAN
*(Sitting down on the floor with others who have
brought food)*
When you come early, you can eat in comfort.

A BURGHER
(Leading his son)
Let's sit here, my son.

A CARD PLAYER

Three aces!

ANOTHER MAN
*(Taking a bottle from under his cloak and sitting
down)*
A drunk should drink his Burgundy . . . *(Drinks.)* . . .
in the House of Burgundy!

THE BURGHER
(To his son)
It's as if we were in some den of evil! *(Points to the
drunkard with his cane.)* Drinkers! *(In stepping back, one
of the fencers jostles him.)* Brawlers! *(He falls in the
midst of the card players.)* Gamblers!

THE GUARDSMAN
(Behind him, still grappling with the FLOWER GIRL*)*
A kiss!

THE BURGHER
(Hurriedly leading his son away)
Good heavens! To think that Rotrou* was performed in
such a place as this, my son!

THE YOUNG MAN
And Corneille!

A BAND OF PAGES
(They enter holding hands, dancing, and singing.)
Tra-la-la-la-la-la-la-la-la-la-la . . .

THE DOORKEEPER
(Sternly, to the PAGES)
Behave yourselves, boys! No pranks!

FIRST PAGE
(With wounded dignity)
Oh, sir, how can you even suspect such a thing? *(With
animation, to the SECOND PAGE, as soon as the DOOR-
KEEPER has turned his back)* Do you have your string?

SECOND PAGE
Yes, and my fishhook.

FIRST PAGE
Good. We'll fish for wigs when we're up there.

A THIEF
*(Gathering several disreputable-looking men around
him)*
Come closer, my young rascals, and let me educate you.
Since you're about to try your hand at stealing for the
first time . . .

SECOND PAGE
(Shouting to other PAGES in the upper gallery)
Hey! Have you brought your peashooters?

THIRD PAGE
Yes! And peas, too!
(Blows peas at them.)

THE YOUNG MAN
(To his father)
What's the name of the play?

* Jean de Rotrou (1609–50), French playwright.

THE BURGHER

La Clorise.

THE YOUNG MAN

Who wrote it?

THE BURGHER

Monsieur Balthazar Baro.* It's a play that . . .
(Walks upstage, holding his son's arm.)

THE THIEF
(To his disciples)
. . . and lace, especially on the legs. Cut it off. . . .

A SPECTATOR
(To another, pointing to a corner of the gallery)
I was up there at the first performance of *The Cid.*

THE THIEF
(Making the gesture of picking a pocket)
Watches . . .

THE BURGHER
(Walking downstage with his son)
You'll see some very famous actors . . .

THE THIEF
*(Making the gesture of furtively and delicately pull-
ing out a handkerchief)*
Handkerchiefs . . .

THE BURGHER
Montfleury, for example . . .

A VOICE FROM THE UPPER GALLERY
Light the chandeliers!

THE BURGHER
. . . Bellerose, L'Epy, La Beaupré, Jodelet!†

---

* Balthazar Baro (1600–50) was a French playwright and novelist
whose dramatic works have now faded into oblivion.

† Bellerose, L'Epy, La Beaupré, and Jodelet, as well as Montfleury, mentioned above, were all French actors of the time in which
the play is set.

A PAGE
(On the floor)
Ah, here's the refreshment girl!

THE REFRESHMENT GIRL
(Appearing behind the refreshment table)
Oranges, milk, raspberry syrup, cider. . . .
(Commotion at the door)

A HIGH-PITCHED VOICE
Out of the way, you brutes!

A LACKEY
(Surprised)
Are there marquis down here on the floor?

ANOTHER LACKEY
Not for long.
(A group of young MARQUIS *enters.)*

A MARQUIS
(Seeing that the theater is half empty)
What's this? We've arrived like tradesmen, without disturbing people, without stepping on their feet? What a shameful way to make an entrance! *(Finds himself in front of some other noblemen who have entered shortly before.)* Cuigy! Brissaille!
(They embrace enthusiastically.)

CUIGY
Ah, the faithful are here! Yes, it's true: we've come before the candles. . . .

THE MARQUIS
No, don't talk about it! I'm so annoyed. . . .

ANOTHER MARQUIS
Cheer up, Marquis, here comes the lighter!

THE CROWD
(Greeting the entrance of the lighter)
Ah! . . .
(Groups form around the chandeliers as he lights them. A few people have taken their places in the galleries. LIGNIÈRE *and* CHRISTIAN DE NEUVILLETTE *enter, arm in arm.* LIGNIÈRE *is rather disheveled, with*

the face of a distinguished drunkard. CHRISTIAN *is
elegantly dressed, but in a somewhat outmoded style.
He seems preoccupied, and looks up at the boxes.)*

Scene II

*The same, with Christian and Lignière, then Ragueneau
and Le Bret.*

CUIGY

Lignière!

BRISSAILLE
(Laughing)
Still sober!

LIGNIÈRE
(Aside, to CHRISTIAN*)*
Shall I introduce you? (CHRISTIAN *nods.*) Baron de
Neuvillette.
(They bow.)

THE CROWD
(Acclaiming the raising of the first lighted chandelier)
Ah!

CUIGY
(To BRISSAILLE, *looking at* CHRISTIAN*)*
He has a charming face!

FIRST MARQUIS
(Disdainfully, having overheard)
Really!

LIGNIÈRE
(Introducing them to CHRISTIAN*)*
Messieurs de Cuigy, de Brissaille. . . .

CHRISTIAN
(Bowing)
Delighted to meet you, gentlemen.

FIRST MARQUIS
(To the second)
He's rather handsome, but he's not dressed in the latest fashion.

LIGNIÈRE
(To CUIGY*)*
Monsieur de Neuvillette has just arrived from Touraine.

CHRISTIAN
Yes, I've been in Paris only three weeks. I'm entering the Guards tomorrow, as a Cadet.

FIRST MARQUIS
(Looking at the people entering the boxes)
There's Madame Aubry, the magistrate's wife!

THE REFRESHMENT GIRL
Oranges, milk. . . .

THE VIOLINISTS
(Tuning their instruments)
La . . . la . . .

CUIGY
(To CHRISTIAN, *pointing to the auditorium, which is beginning to fill)*
People are arriving.

CHRISTIAN
Yes, in droves!

FIRST MARQUIS
All of fashionable society is here!
(They name the richly dressed ladies as they enter the boxes, bowing to them and receiving smiles in return.)
3.5SECOND MARQUIS
Mesdames de Guéméné . . .

CUIGY
De Bois-Dauphin . . .

FIRST MARQUIS
Whom we have loved . . .

BRISSAILLE
De Chavigny . . .

SECOND MARQUIS

Who plays with our hearts!

LIGNIÈRE

I see Monsieur de Corneille has come from Rouen.

THE YOUNG MAN

(To his father)
Is the Academy* here?

THE BURGHER

I see several members. There's Boudu, and Boissat, and
Cureau de la Chambre; Porchères, Colomby, Bourzeys,
Bourdon, Arbaud. . . . All those names that will never
die! It's awesome to see such men!

FIRST MARQUIS

Look, our lady intellectuals are taking their places: Barthénoïde, Urimédonte, Cassandace, Félixérie. . . .

SECOND MARQUIS

(Ecstatically)
Dear God, but their surnames are exquisite! Marquis,
do you know them all?

FIRST MARQUIS

I know them all, Marquis!

LIGNIÈRE

(Taking CHRISTIAN aside)
My friend, I came with you to help you, but since the
lady isn't here I'll return to my vice.

CHRISTIAN

(Imploringly)
No, stay! You know everyone at court and in the city:
you'll be able to tell me the name of the lady for whom
I'm dying of love.

---

* The French Academy, founded in 1635 and still in existence.
Its membership is limited to forty of the most distinguished French
writers. The men named below (Boudu, Boissat, etc.) were among
its earlier members.

THE FIRST VIOLINIST
(Rapping on his desk with his bow)
Ready, gentlemen. . . .
(Raises his bow.)

THE REFRESHMENT GIRL
Macaroons, lemonade. . . .
(The violins begin playing.)

CHRISTIAN
I'm afraid she may be coquettish and refined. I don't
dare to speak to her, because I have no wit. I don't
know how to use the elegant language that's in style
nowadays. I'm only a soldier, a shy soldier. . . . She
always sits in that box—there, on the right. It's still
empty. . . .

LIGNIÈRE
(Preparing to leave)
I'm going.

CHRISTIAN
(Holding him back)
Oh, no! Stay!

LIGNIÈRE
I can't. D'Assoucy is waiting for me at the tavern. A
man could die of thirst here!

THE REFRESHMENT GIRL
(Passing in front of him with a tray)
Orangeade?

LIGNIÈRE
Bah!

THE REFRESHMENT GIRL
Milk?

LIGNIÈRE
Are you trying to make me sick?

THE REFRESHMENT GIRL
White wine?

LIGNIÈRE
Aha! *(To* CHRISTIAN*)* I'll stay a little longer, since you

insist. (*To the* REFRESHMENT GIRL) Now, about that
white wine. . . .
 *(He sits down near the refreshment table and she
 pours him a glass of wine.)*

VOICES FROM THE CROWD
 *(Greeting the entrance of a plump, jolly-looking lit-
 tle man)*
Ah, Ragueneau!

LIGNIÈRE
 (To CHRISTIAN*)*
There's Ragueneau, the great baker.

RAGUENEAU
 *(Dressed like a pastry cook in his Sunday best, hur-
 rying toward* LIGNIÈRE*)*
Sir, have you seen Monsieur de Cyrano?

LIGNIÈRE
 (Introducing RAGUENEAU *to* CHRISTIAN*)*
This is Ragueneau, the pastry cook of actors and poets!

RAGUENEAU
 (Embarrassed)
You honor me too highly.

LIGNIÈRE
Not at all! You're a patron of the arts!

RAGUENEAU
Poets do come to my shop . . .

LIGNIÈRE
To buy on credit. And you yourself are a talented poet.

RAGUENEAU
So I've been told.

LIGNIÈRE
You're madly in love with poetry!

RAGUENEAU
It's true that for an ode . . .

LIGNIÈRE
You give a tart.

RAGUENEAU

Only a little one, if it's a short ode.

LIGNIÈRE

No need to apologize! Such modesty! And what do you give for a triolet?

RAGUENEAU

Rolls.

LIGNIÈRE

(Sternly)
Rolls of the very highest quality. You love the theater, too, don't you?

RAGUENEAU

I adore it.

LIGNIÈRE

You pay for your theater tickets with pastry! Tell me, just between ourselves, how much did you pay this time?

RAGUENEAU

Four custard tarts and fifteen cream puffs. *(Looks all around.)* Monsieur de Cyrano isn't here? I'm surprised.

LIGNIÈRE

Why?

RAGUENEAU

Montfleury is in the play!

LIGNIÈRE

Yes, that walking barrel will play the part of Phaedo today. But what does it matter to Cyrano?

RAGUENEAU

Haven't you heard? He took a dislike to Montfleury and ordered him not to appear on the stage for a month.

LIGNIÈRE

(Who has by now taken his fourth glass of wine)
Well, what of it?

RAGUENEAU

Montfleury is in the play!

CUIGY
(Who has joined the group)
There's nothing he can do about it.

RAGUENEAU
Ah, that's what I've come to see!

FIRST MARQUIS
Who is this Cyrano?

CUIGY
He's a man who knows how to handle a rapier.

SECOND MARQUIS
A nobleman?

CUIGY
Noble enough. He's a Cadet* in the Guards. *(Points to a gentleman who is walking back and forth as though looking for someone.)* But his friend Le Bret can tell you. . . . *(Calls him.)* Le Bret! (LE BRET *comes over to them.)* You're looking for Bergerac?

LE BRET
Yes, and I'm worried. . . .

CUIGY
He's an extraordinary man, isn't he?

LE BRET
(Affectionately)
The most delightful man under the sun!

RAGUENEAU
A poet!

CUIGY
A swordsman!

BRISSAILLE
A scientist!

LE BRET
A musician!

---

* In seventeenth-century France, a Cadet was a nobleman serving as a common soldier or noncommissioned officer in order to acquire military experience and knowledge that he would later use as an officer.

LIGNIÈRE

And what an uncommon appearance!

RAGUENEAU

Yes, I doubt that the solemn Philippe de Champaigne will ever paint him for us. But odd, impetuous, brash, and outlandish as he is, proudest of all the thin-skinned swaggerers lovingly spawned by Gascony, I think he would have given the late Jacques Callot a wild swashbuckler to place among his portraits. With his triple-plumed hat, his billowing doublet, and his cape majestically held out behind by a sword that rises like the insolent tail of a cock, he carries his nose above a punchinello ruff, a nose that . . . Ah, gentlemen, what a nose! Those who see it pass by can't help exclaiming, "No, it can't be true!" Then they smile and say, "He'll soon take it off." But Monsieur de Bergerac never takes it off.

LE BRET

(Nodding)

He keeps it on—and runs his sword through anyone who looks at it too closely.

RAGUENEAU

(Proudly)

His blade is half the shears of Fate!

FIRST MARQUIS

(Shrugging)

He won't come.

RAGUENEAU

He will! I'll bet you a chicken à la Ragueneau!

FIRST MARQUIS

(Laughing)

I'll take that bet!

(Murmurs of admiration from the crowd: ROXANE *has just appeared in her box. She sits at the front of it, her* DUENNA *sits at the rear.* CHRISTIAN, *occupied in paying the* REFRESHMENT GIRL, *has not yet seen her.)*

SECOND MARQUIS

(With little cries)
Gentlemen, she's terrifyingly lovely!

FIRST MARQUIS

Skin like a peach, smiling with strawberry lips!

SECOND MARQUIS

And so fresh and cool that anyone coming near her might catch a cold in his heart!

CHRISTIAN

(Looks up, sees ROXANE, *and clutches* LIGNIÈRE'S *arm.)*
There she is!

LIGNIÈRE

(Looking)
Ah, so she's the one?

CHRISTIAN

Yes. Quickly, tell me who she is! I'm afraid.

LIGNIÈRE

(Still sipping his wine)
Magdeleine Robin, known as Roxane. Sharp-witted, an intellectual . . .

CHRISTIAN

Alas!

LIGNIÈRE

. . . free, an orphan, a cousin of Cyrano, whom we were just discussing. . . .
(At this point a very elegant gentleman, wearing the Cordon Bleu around his neck, enters ROXANE'S *box and stands talking with her for a few moments.)*

CHRISTIAN

(Starting)
Who is that man?

LIGNIÈRE

(Winking, beginning to show the effects of the wine)
That, my friend, is Count de Guiche. He's in love with her, but he's married to Cardinal Richelieu's niece. He wants to arrange a marriage between Roxane and Vis-

count de Valvert, a sad specimen of a man whom he
can count on to be obliging. She's opposed to it, but De
Guiche is powerful: he can persecute an untitled girl like
her. Incidentally, I've written a song exposing his crafty
scheme. He must hate me for it! The ending is positively
vicious. Listen, I'll sing it for you. . . .
  *(He rises unsteadily to his feet and holds up his glass,
  ready to sing.)*

CHRISTIAN

No. I'm leaving now.

LIGNIÈRE

Where are you going?

CHRISTIAN

I'm going to pay a visit to Viscount de Valvert!

LIGNIÈRE

Don't do anything rash: there's a good chance he'd kill
you. *(Discreetly calls his attention to* ROXANE.*)* Stay.
You're being watched.

CHRISTIAN

It's true!
  *(He stands staring at her. Seeing him looking up with
  his mouth open, the* THIEF *and his accomplices begin
  moving toward him.)*

LIGNIÈRE

I'm the one who's leaving. I'm thirsty and I have an
appointment—in a tavern!
  (He staggers out.)

LE BRET

  (With relief, coming back to RAGUENEAU *after having searched everywhere)*
No sign of Cyrano.

RAGUENEAU

  (Incredulously)
It doesn't seem possible.

LE BRET

I'm hoping he hasn't seen the poster.

THE CROWD

Begin the play! Begin!

Scene III

The same, except for Lignière; De Guiche, Valvert, then Montfleury.

A MARQUIS
(Watching DE GUICHE *come down from* ROXANE'S *box and walk across the floor, surrounded by obsequious noblemen, one of whom is* VISCOUNT DE VALVERT*)*
De Guiche has his own little court!

SECOND MARQUIS
(With distaste)
Another Gascon!

FIRST MARQUIS
Yes, but a flexible, calculating Gascon—the kind who succeeds! We'd better go and pay our respects to him, take my word for it.
(They approach DE GUICHE.*)*

SECOND MARQUIS
What beautiful ribbons, Monsieur de Guiche! What would you call that color? Is it "Kiss-me-my-darling," or is it "Doe's-belly?"

DE GUICHE
I call it "Sick Spaniard."

FIRST MARQUIS
An appropriate name, because soon, thanks to your valor, the Spaniards in Flanders* will be in very sickly condition!

DE GUICHE
I'm going to sit on the stage. Are you coming with me?
(He walks toward the stage, followed by all the MARQUIS *and other noblemen, then looks back and calls.)* Come, Valvert!
*(*CHRISTIAN *has been observing and listening to them. He starts when he hears* VALVERT'S *name.)*

* At the time of the play the French were fighting the Spanish for possession of Flanders, then part of the Spanish Netherlands.

CHRISTIAN

Valvert! I'll throw my glove in his face this instant!
*(Reaches for his gloves and encounters the hand of a thief
picking his pocket. Turns around.)* What . . .

THE THIEF

Oh, no!

CHRISTIAN
   (Holding him)
I was reaching for a glove!

THE THIEF
   (With a pitiful smile)
You found a hand instead. *(Lowering his voice and
speaking rapidly)* Let me go and I'll tell you a secret.

CHRISTIAN
   (Still holding him)
What is it?

THE THIEF

Lignière, who just left you . . .

CHRISTIAN
   (Without letting go of him)
Yes? Go on.

THE THIEF

He's about to meet his death. He wrote a song that
offended a certain very powerful person, and tonight a
hundred men—I know, because I'm to join them soon—
have been posted . . .

CHRISTIAN

A hundred! By whom?

THE THIEF

Sorry, I can't tell you that.

CHRISTIAN
   (Shrugging)
Oh, come, come!

THE THIEF
   (With great dignity)
It's a professional secret!

CHRISTIAN

Where are the men posted?

THE THIEF

At the Porte de Nesle, on his way. Warn him!

CHRISTIAN
(Finally letting go of him)
But how can I find him?

THE THIEF

Hurry to all his favorite taverns—the Golden Winepress, the Pine Cone, the Breaking Belt, the Two Torches, the Three Funnels—and leave a note for him in each of them.

CHRISTIAN

Yes, I'll go! Oh, the vile cowards! A hundred men against one! *(Looks at* ROXANE *with love.)* How can I bear to leave her? *(At* VALVERT *with fury)* And him! But I must save Lignière!
(He runs out. DE GUICHE, VALVERT, *the* MARQUIS, *and the other noblemen have disappeared behind the curtain to take their places on the benches on the stage. The floor, the gallery, and the boxes are now completely filled.)*

THE CROWD

Begin the play!

A BURGHER
(Whose wig has just been hooked and lifted at the end of a string by a PAGE *in the upper gallery)*
My wig!

JOYOUS SHOUTS

He's bald!—Good work, page!—Ha! ha! ha!

THE BURGHER
(Angrily shaking his fist)
You young bandit!

LAUGHTER AND SHOUTS
(Beginning loudly, then dying away)
Ha! ha! ha! ha! ha! ha!
(Complete silence)

LE BRET
(Astonished)
Why this sudden silence? *(A* SPECTATOR *speaks to him in an undertone.)* Oh?

THE SPECTATOR
Yes, it was just told to me by someone who knows for certain.

MURMURS
(All through the crowd)
Sh!—Is it true?—No!—Yes!—In the grilled box.—The Cardinal!—The Cardinal?—The Cardinal!

A PAGE
That means the end of all our fun!
(Three raps are heard from the stage. Everyone becomes motionless and waits.)

THE VOICE OF A MARQUIS
(In the silence, from behind the curtain)
Put out that candle!

ANOTHER MARQUIS
(Putting his head between the two halves of the curtain)
A chair!
(A chair is passed from hand to hand, above the heads of the audience. The MARQUIS *takes it and disappears, after throwing a few kisses to the boxes.)*

A SPECTATOR
Silence!
(Three more raps from the stage. The curtain opens. Tableau. The MARQUIS *are seated on either side of the stage in insolent poses. The backdrop represents a bluish pastoral scene. Four small crystal chandeliers light the stage. The violins are playing softly.)*

LE BRET
(To RAGUENEAU, *in a low voice)*
Will Montfleury soon be on the stage?

RAGUENEAU
(Also in a low voice)
He'll be the first to appear.

LE BRET
Cyrano isn't here.

RAGUENEAU
I've lost my bet.

LE BRET
So much the better!
(A bagpipe melody is heard, then the enormously fat
MONTFLEURY *appears on the stage, wearing a shepherd's costume, a hat adorned with roses tilted over one ear, blowing into a beribboned bagpipe.)*

THE CROWD
(Applauding)
Montfleury!—Bravo!—Montfleury!

MONTFLEURY
(After bowing, playing the part of Phaedo)
"Happy is he who shuns the pomp of courts
In solitary exile, self-imposed;
And who, when gentle breezes . . ."

A VOICE
(From the middle of the floor)
Haven't I ordered you off the stage for a month, you wretched scoundrel?
(Astonishment in the audience. Everyone looks around. Murmurs.)

VARIOUS VOICES
Oh!—What!—Who?
(Those in the boxes stand up to see.)

CUIGY
He's here!

LE BRET
(Terrified)
Cyrano!

THE VOICE
Off the stage this instant, king of buffoons!

THE WHOLE AUDIENCE
(Indignantly)

Oh!

MONTFLEURY

But . . .

THE VOICE

You refuse?

VARIOUS VOICES
(From the floor and the boxes)

Sh!—Enough!—Go on, Montfleury!—Don't be afraid!

MONTFLEURY
(In a faltering voice)

"Happy is he who shuns the pomp of . . ."

THE VOICE
(More threateningly)

Well, prince of louts, must I give your shoulders a taste
of wood?
*(An arm holding a cane rises above the heads of
the audience.)*

MONTFLEURY
(In an increasingly feeble voice)

"Happy is he who . . ."
(The arm waves the cane.)

THE VOICE

Off the stage!

THE CROWD

Oh!

MONTFLEURY
(Choking)

"Happy is he who shuns . . ."

CYRANO
*(Standing up on a chair with his arms folded, his hat
cocked, his mustache bristling, and his nose pointing aggressively)*

I'm about to lose my temper!
(His appearance creates a sensation.)

Scene IV

The same, with Cyrano, then Bellerose and Jodelet.

MONTFLEURY
(To the MARQUIS*)*
Protect me, gentlemen!

A MARQUIS
(Nonchalantly)
Go on with your acting.

CYRANO
If you do, you fat oaf, I'll tan your cheeks!

THE MARQUIS
Enough!

CYRANO
(To all the MARQUIS*)*
I advise you all to sit quietly in your seats. Otherwise
my cane will rumple your ribbons!

ALL THE MARQUIS
(Standing)
This is too much!—Montfleury . . .

CYRANO
Montfleury will leave, if he doesn't want his ears clipped
and his belly slit open!

A VOICE
But . . .

CYRANO
He will leave!

ANOTHER VOICE
You can't . . .

CYRANO
Still there? *(Makes the gesture of rolling up his sleeves.)*
Very well, then, I'll go up on the stage and carve that
thick sausage into thin slices.

MONTFLEURY
(Gathering all his dignity)
In insulting me, sir, you insult the Dramatic Muse!

CYRANO
You are a stranger to that Muse, sir, but if she ever had
the honor of meeting you, the sight of your fat, stupid
face would inspire her to give you a vigorous kick in the
broadest part of your anatomy!

THE CROWD
Montfleury!—Montfleury!—Baro's play!

CYRANO
(To those shouting around him)
Please have pity on my sword: if you don't stop shouting
you'll frighten it out of its scabbard.
(The circle widens.)

THE CROWD
(Retreating)
Make room!—Step back!

CYRANO
(To MONTFLEURY*)*
Off the stage! *(The crowd closes in with an angry mur-
mur. He quickly turns around.)* Is there something you
want to say to me? Speak up!
(The crowd retreats again.)

A VOICE
(Singing from the back of the room)
Monsieur de Cyrano
Is arrogant today;
His tyranny must go:
We've come to see the play!

THE WHOLE AUDIENCE
(Singing)
The play! The play! . . .

CYRANO
If I hear any more of that song, I'll break every head in
this theater!

A BURGHER

You're not Samson!

CYRANO

I can do as well as he, sir, if you'll be so kind as to lend me your jawbone.

A LADY

(In the boxes)
This is incredible!

A NOBLEMAN

Scandalous!

A BURGHER

Exasperating!

A PAGE

Hilarious!

THE CROWD

Montfleury!—Cyrano!

CYRANO

Silence!

THE CROWD

(Uproariously)
Hee-haw!—Baa!—Woof, woof!—Cock-a-doodle-doo!

CYRANO

Quiet, or I'll . . .

A PAGE

Meow!

CYRANO

I order you to be silent! And I issue a collective challenge! Come, I'll write down your names. Step forward, young heroes! You'll all have a turn, I'll give each of you a number. Now, who wants to be at the top of the list? You, sir? No? You? No? I'll dispatch the first duelist with all the honors that are his due. All of you who want to die, hold up your hands. *(Silence)* Does modesty forbid you to look at my naked sword? No names? No hands? . . . Then I'll get on with my business. *(He turns back toward the stage, where* MONTFLEURY *has been wait-*

ing in great anxiety.) I want to see the theater cured of
this boil. Otherwise . . . *(Puts his hand to his sword.)* . . .
I'll lance it!

MONTFLEURY

I . . .

CYRANO
*(Descends from his chair, sits down in the middle of
the circle that has formed around him, and settles
himself as though at home.)*
I'm going to clap my hands three times. By the third
clap, you will be gone.

THE CROWD
(Amused)
Ah!

CYRANO
(Clapping his hands)
One!

MONTFLEURY

I . . .

A VOICE
(From the boxes)
Stay!

THE CROWD
He'll stay—He'll go!

MONTFLEURY
Gentlemen, I believe . . .

CYRANO
Two!

MONTFLEURY
I'm sure it would be better . . .

CYRANO
Three!
*(MONTFLEURY suddenly disappears. Storm of laugh-
ter, hisses, and boos.)*

THE CROWD
Boo!—Boo!—Coward!—Come back!

CYRANO
(Leans back in his chair, beaming, and crosses his legs.)
Let him come back if he dares!

A BURGHER
Here's the spokesman of the troupe!
(BELLEROSE comes forward and bows.)

THE BOXES
Ah!—Here's Bellerose!

BELLEROSE
(Elegantly)
Noble lords . . .

THE CROWD
No! No! Jodelet!

JODELET
(In a nasal voice, stepping forward)
Miserable clods!

THE CROWD
Ah!—Ah!—Bravo!—Very good!—Bravo!

JODELET
No bravos! Our beloved bulky tragedian has had a sudden . . .

THE CROWD
He's a coward!

JODELET
He had to leave!

THE CROWD
Call him back!

SEVERAL VOICES
No!

OTHER VOICES
Yes!

A YOUNG MAN
(To CYRANO)
Tell me, sir, what reason do you have to hate Montfleury?

CYRANO

(Graciously, still seated)

I have two reasons, my callow young friend, either of
which would be sufficient. The first is that he's a deplor-
able actor who brays like an ass and wrestles ponder-
ously with lines that ought to soar lightly from his lips.
The second—is my secret.

THE OLD BURGHER

(Behind him)

But you're high-handedly depriving us of *La Clorise*!
I insist . . .

CYRANO

(Respectfully, turning his chair toward the BURGHER*)*

Sir, your pigheadedness can't change the fact that old
Baro's verse is worthless. I feel no remorse at having
deprived you of trash.

THE LADY INTELLECTUALS

(In the boxes)

Oh!—Our Baro!—My dear, it's . . . How dare he!—
Such insolence!

CYRANO

(Gallantly, turning his chair toward the boxes)

Fair ladies, blossom and be radiant, fill our dreams with
longing, soften death with a smile, inspire poetry—but
don't judge it!

BELLEROSE

What about the money that will have to be refunded?

CYRANO

(Turning his chair toward the stage)

Now there's the first sensible thing that's yet been said!
Far be it from me to impose hardship on practitioners
of the Thespian art. *(Stands up and throws a bag onto
the stage.)* Here, take this purse and be quiet.

THE CROWD

(Astonished)

Ah!—Oh!

JODELET

(Quickly picking up the purse and weighing it in his hand)

At this price, sir, I'll be glad to have you come and stop our performance every day!

THE CROWD

Boo! Boo!

JODELET

Even if we must all be booed together!

BELLEROSE

Please clear the hall!

JODELET

Everyone out, please!

(The spectators begin leaving while CYRANO watches with satisfaction, but they soon stop when they hear the following scene. The ladies in the boxes, who have already stood up and put on their cloaks, stop to listen, and finally sit down again.)

LE BRET

(To CYRANO)

This is madness!

A MEDDLER

(Who has approached CYRANO)

What a scandal! Montfleury, the great actor! Don't you know he's protected by the Duke de Candale? Do you have a patron?

CYRANO

No!

THE MEDDLER

You don't have a . . .

CYRANO

No!

THE MEDDLER

What? You have no great lord whose name protects . . .

CYRANO

(Annoyed)
For the third time, no! Must I say it a fourth? I don't
rely on some remote patron for protection. *(Puts his
hand to his sword.)* My protector is always near at hand.

THE MEDDLER
Are you going to leave the city?

CYRANO
That depends.

THE MEDDLER
But the Duke de Candale has a long arm!

CYRANO
Not as long as mine . . . *(Pointing to his sword)* . . .
when I give it this extension!

THE MEDDLER
But surely you wouldn't dare . . .

CYRANO
I would.

THE MEDDLER
But . . .

CYRANO
Go now.

THE MEDDLER
But . . .

CYRANO
Go! Or tell me why you're looking at my nose.

THE MEDDLER
(Petrified)
I . . .

CYRANO
(Moving toward him)
Do you find it surprising?

THE MEDDLER
(Stepping back)
You're mistaken, my lord. . . .

CYRANO

Is it limp and dangling, like an elephant's trunk?

THE MEDDLER
(Stepping back again)

I didn't . . .

CYRANO

Or hooked like an owl's beak?

THE MEDDLER

I . . .

CYRANO

Do you see a wart at the end of it?

THE MEDDLER

I . . .

CYRANO

Or a fly walking on it? What's unusual about it?

THE MEDDLER

Nothing, I . . .

CYRANO

Is it a startling sight?

THE MEDDLER

Sir, I've been careful not to look at it!

CYRANO

Would you please tell me why?

THE MEDDLER

I was . . .

CYRANO

Does it disgust you?

THE MEDDLER

Sir . . .

CYRANO

Does its color seem unhealthy to you?

THE MEDDLER

Sir!

CYRANO

Is its shape obscene?

THE MEDDLER

Not at all!

CYRANO

Then why that disdainful expression? Do you find it, perhaps, a little too large?

THE MEDDLER

(Stammering)

Oh, no, it's quite small . . . very small . . . diminutive. . . .

CYRANO

What! How dare you accuse me of anything so ridiculous? A small nose? *My* nose? You've gone too far!

THE MEDDLER

Please, sir, I . . .

CYRANO

My nose is *enormous,* you snub-nosed, flat-faced wretch! I carry it with pride, because a big nose is a sign of affability, kindness, courtesy, wit, generosity, and courage. I have all those qualities, but you can never hope to have any of them, since the ignoble face that my hand is about to meet above your collar . . . *(Slaps him. The* MEDDLER *cries out in pain.)* . . . has no more glory, nobility, poetry, quaintness, vivacity, or grandeur—no more *nose,* in short—than the face that my boot . . . *(Turns him around by the shoulders.)* . . . is about to meet below your waist!

(Kicks him.)

THE MEDDLER

(Running away)

Help! Guards!

CYRANO

Let that be a lesson to anyone else who may feel that the middle of my face is amusing. If the joker is a nobleman, I deal with him a little differently. I administer his punishment from the front, and higher up, and not with leather, but with steel.

DE GUICHE

*(Who has come down from the seats on the stage,
with the MARQUIS)*
He's beginning to be annoying!

VALVERT

(Shrugging)
He likes to bluster.

DE GUICHE

Isn't anyone going to silence him?

VALVERT

Yes, *I* will! Just watch his face when he hears what I
have to say to him! *(Walks up to CYRANO, who observes
him, and stands in front of him with a fatuous expression.)* You have a nose that . . . Your nose is . . . um . . .
very big.

CYRANO

(Gravely)
Yes, very.

VALVERT

(Laughing)
Ha!

CYRANO

(With perfect calm)
Is that all?

VALVERT

Well . . .

CYRANO

I'm afraid your speech was a little short, young man.
You could have said . . . oh, all sorts of things, varying
your tone to fit your words. Let me give you a few
examples.

In an aggressive tone: "If I had a nose like that, I'd
have it amputated!"

Friendly: "The end of it must get wet when you drink
from a cup. Why don't you use a tankard?"

Descriptive: "It's a rock, a peak, a cape! No, more
than a cape: a peninsula!"

Curious: "What do you use that long container for? Do you keep your pens and scissors in it?"

Gracious: "What a kind man you are! You love birds so much that you've given them a perch to roost on."

Truculent: "When you light your pipe and the smoke comes out your nose, the neighbors must think a chimney has caught fire!"

Solicitous: "Be careful when you walk: with all that weight on your head, you could easily lose your balance and fall."

Thoughtful: "You ought to put an awning over it, to keep its color from fading in the sun."

Pedantic: "Sir, only the animal that Aristophanes calls the hippocampelephantocamelos could have had so much flesh and bone below its forehead."

Flippant: "That tusk must be convenient to hang your hat on."

Grandiloquent: "No wind but the mighty Arctic blast, majestic nose, could ever give you a cold from one end to the other!"

Dramatic: "When it bleeds, it must be like the Red Sea!"

Admiring: "What a sign for a perfume shop!"

Lyrical: "Is that a conch, and are you Triton risen from the sea?"

Naïve: "Is that monument open to the public?"

Respectful: "One look at your face, sir, is enough to tell me that you are indeed a man of substance."

Rustic: "That don't look like no nose to me. It's either a big cucumber or a little watermelon."

Military: "The enemy is charging! Aim your cannon!"

Practical: "A nose like that has one advantage: it keeps your feet dry in the rain."

Or finally, parodying the grief-stricken Pyramus in Théophile de Viau's play: "This nose destroyed the harmony of its good master's features! See how the traitor blushes now for shame!"*

---

* The reference is to a line from the play *Pyrame et Thisbé* by Théophile de Viau (1590–1626): "Here is the dagger that basely sullied itself with its master's blood. It is red with shame, the traitor!"

There, now you have an inkling of what you might
have said to me if you were witty and a man of letters.
Unfortunately you're totally witless and a man of very
few letters: only the four that spell the word "fool." But
even if you had the intelligence to invent remarks like
those I've given you as examples, you would not have
been able to entertain me with them. You would have
spoken no more than half the first syllable of the first
word, because such jesting is a privilege that I grant only
to myself.

DE GUICHE
(Trying to lead away the outraged VALVERT*)*
Come, never mind.

VALVERT
(Choking with anger)
Such arrogance from an uncouth barbarian who . . .
who . . . isn't even wearing gloves! Who appears in public without ribbons, or tassels, or braid!

CYRANO
I have a different idea of elegance. I don't dress like a
fop, it's true, but my moral grooming is impeccable. I
never appear in public with a soiled conscience, a tarnished honor, threadbare scruples, or an insult that I
haven't washed away. I'm always immaculately clean,
adorned with independence and frankness. I may not cut
a stylish figure, but I hold my soul erect. I wear my
deeds as ribbons, my wit is sharper than the finest mustache, and when I walk among men I make truths ring
like spurs.

VALVERT
You . . .

CYRANO
I have no gloves? It doesn't trouble me. I had a pair not
long ago, but I lost one of them, so I threw the other
one away—in someone's face.

VALVERT
Stupid lout, insolent boor, ridiculous ass!

CYRANO
(Taking off his hat and bowing as though VALVERT *had just introduced himself)*
Delighted to meet you. I'm Savinien de Cyrano de Bergerac.
(Laughter)

VALVERT
(Exasperated)
Buffoon!

CYRANO
(Crying out as if in pain)
Oh!

VALVERT
(Turning back, after having turned away)
What's he saying now?

CYRANO
(With a grimace of pain)
I must move it: it's fallen asleep. It needs exercise. Oh!

VALVERT
What's the matter?

CYRANO
I have a cramp in my sword.

VALVERT
(Drawing his own)
So be it!

CYRANO
I'll give you a charming little thrust.

VALVERT
(Contemptuously)
Poet!

CYRANO
Yes, sir, I *am* a poet, as I'll demonstrate by composing an impromptu ballade while I fence with you.

VALVERT
A ballade?

CYRANO

You don't know what that is? Allow me to explain.

VALVERT

But . . .

CYRANO

(As though reciting a lesson)
The ballade consists of three eight-line stanzas . . .

VALVERT

(Stamping his foot)
Oh!

CYRANO

(Continuing)
. . . with a four-line refrain at the end.

VALVERT

You . . .

CYRANO

I'm going to compose one as I fight with you, and when
I come to the last line, I'll draw blood.

VALVERT

No!

CYRANO

No? Wait and see. *(Declaiming)* "Ballade of the Duel
between Monsieur de Bergerac and an Imbecile, in the
Hôtel de Bourgogne."

VALVERT

What's all that?

CYRANO

It's the title.

THE CROWD

(Greatly excited)
Make room!—This will be worth seeing!—Step back!—
Quiet!
*(Tableau. A circle of onlookers on the floor, with
MARQUIS and OFFICERS mingled with BURGHERS and
less affluent commoners. The PAGES have climbed up
on men's shoulders to see better. All the women are*

standing in their boxes. To the right, DE GUICHE *and his gentlemen; to the left,* LE BRET, RAGUENEAU, CUIGY, *etc.)*

CYRANO
(Closing his eyes for a moment)
Wait, I'm thinking of how to begin. . . . There, I have it.
(His actions match his words throughout the ballade.)
I take off my hat and discard it,
I slowly abandon my cloak,
I draw my sword out of its scabbard,
Preparing to put it to use.
For the moment, I stand here before you,
Elegant, calm, and serene,
But I warn you, my impudent scoundrel,
When I end the refrain, I draw blood.

(They begin fencing.)

You should have avoided this battle.
Now, where shall I skewer you, goose?
In the side, 'neath the sleeve of your doublet?
In the heart, 'neath the ribbon you wear?
No, I've carefully thought and reflected,
And finally made up my mind;
The paunch: that's where I've decided,
When I end the refrain, to draw blood.

I see you give ground when I press you;
Your face is as white as a sheet;
Is "coward" a name that would suit you?
I dexterously parry the point
That you hoped to thrust into my entrails;
Your efforts are doomed to be vain.
Prepare yourself now to be punctured:
When I end the refrain, I draw blood.

(Announces solemnly.)

Refrain:
Pray God to forgive your transgressions!
The close of our combat draws near;
A coupé, then a feint, then the finish!

(He lunges. VALVERT *staggers.* CYRANO *bows.)*
When I end the refrain, I draw blood.

(Cheers. Applause from the boxes. Flowers and handkerchiefs are thrown down. Officers surround and congratulate CYRANO. RAGUENEAU *dances with delight.* LE BRET *is both happy and appalled.* VALVERT's *friends lead him away, holding him up.)*

THE CROWD
(In a long cry)
Ah! . . .

A LIGHT-HORSEMAN
Magnificent!

A WOMAN
Charming!

RAGUENEAU
Phenomenal!

A MARQUIS
Unheard of!

LE BRET
Foolhardy!

THE CROWD
(Swarming around CYRANO*)*
Congratulations!—My compliments!—Bravo!

A WOMAN'S VOICE
He's a hero!

A MUSKETEER
(Walking rapidly toward CYRANO *with his hand outstretched)*
Allow me to shake your hand, sir! It was a superb exploit, and I believe I can claim to be a judge of such things. It made me stamp my feet with joy!
(Walks away.)

CYRANO
(To CUIGY*)*
What is that gentleman's name?

CUIGY

D'Artagnan.*

LE BRET
(To CYRANO, *taking his arm)*
I'd like to have a talk with you.

CYRANO

Wait till this crowd thins out a little. *(To* BELLEROSE*)*
May I stay?

BELLEROSE
(Respectfully)
Of course, sir!
(Shouts are heard from outside.)

JODELET
(Who has gone to look)
Montfleury is being booed!

BELLEROSE

(Solemnly)
Sic transit! . . . *(Changing his tone, to the* DOORKEEPER
and the man who is preparing to put out the candles)
Sweep out the theater and lock the door, but leave the
candles burning. We'll come back after dinner to re-
hearse the new farce we're going to present tomorrow.
*(*JODELET *and* BELLEROSE *go out, after bowing
deeply to* CYRANO.*)*

THE DOORKEEPER
(To CYRANO*)*
Aren't you going to dine, sir?

CYRANO

No.
(The DOORKEEPER *withdraws.)*

LE BRET
(To CYRANO*)*
Why not?

* Charles de Baatz, Seigneur d'Artagnan (1611–73), an officer
who had an outstanding military career. The fictional hero of Alexandre Dumas's *The Three Musketeers* bears d'Artagnan's name and
is modeled on him to a certain extent.

CYRANO

(Proudly)
Because . . . *(Changing his tone, seeing that the* DOOR-
KEEPER *is out of earshot)* Because I have no money.

LE BRET

(Making the gesture of throwing a bag)
What! That bag of money . . .

CYRANO

Alas, my month's allotment lived only for a day!

LE BRET

And for the rest of the month . . .

CYRANO

I have nothing left.

LE BRET

What foolishness to throw it all away!

CYRANO

Yes, but what a gesture!

THE REFRESHMENT GIRL

(Coughing from behind her little counter)
Ahem! . . . (CYRANO *and* LE BRET *turn around. She comes
forward timidly.)* Sir, I . . . I can't bear to think of you
going hungry. *(Points to the refreshment table.)* I have
plenty of food here. . . . *(Wholeheartedly)* Take whatever
you like!

CYRANO

(Gallantly taking off his hat)
My dear child, my Gascon pride forbids me to accept
the slightest morsel from your fingers, but since I fear a
refusal would offend you, I will accept . . . *(Goes to the
refreshment table and chooses.)* Oh, very little! One of
these grapes . . . *(She tries to give him the whole cluster;
he picks off a single grape.)* Only one! . . . This glass of
water . . . *(She tries to pour him a glass of wine; he stops
her.)* And half a macaroon. *(Breaks one and gives her
back the other half.)*

LE BRET

But that's ridiculous!

THE REFRESHMENT GIRL

Oh, please take something else!

CYRANO

I will. Your lovely hand.
(She holds out her hand to him and he kisses it as if she were a princess.)

THE REFRESHMENT GIRL

Thank you, sir. *(Bows.)* Good-by. *(Leaves.)*

Scene V

Cyrano, Le Bret, then the Doorkeeper.

CYRANO

(To LE BRET*)*
You wanted to have a talk with me? I'm ready to listen. *(Sets the macaroon down on the refreshment table in front of him.)* My dinner! . . . *(Sets down the glass of water.)* My drink! . . . *(And finally the grape)* My dessert! *(Sits down.)* There, I'm ready to begin. I have an excellent appetite this evening. *(Eating)* What was it you wanted to tell me?

LE BRET

That you're going to have some badly distorted ideas if you listen only to those fools who like to give themselves such warlike airs. Talk with a few sensible people and you'll be better informed of the effect produced by your act of bravado.

CYRANO

(Finishing his macaroon)
It was enormous.

LE BRET

The Cardinal . . .

CYRANO

(Beaming)
The Cardinal was there?

LE BRET

Yes, and he must have found it . . .

CYRANO

Highly original, I'm sure.

LE BRET

But . . .

CYRANO

He's an author himself. He couldn't have been displeased to see another author's play disrupted.

LE BRET

You've made too many enemies!

CYRANO

About how many would you say I made today?

LE BRET

Forty-eight. Without counting the women.

CYRANO

(Beginning to eat his grape)
Really? That many?

LE BRET

Yes. First, there's Montfleury, then the burgher you kicked, De Guiche, Valvert, of course, Baro, the Academy . . .

CYRANO

Stop! That's already enough to delight me!

LE BRET

I don't understand the way you live. Where will it lead you? What are you trying to accomplish?

CYRANO

I was once confused and bewildered by all the complicated courses of action that were open to me. Finally I chose . . .

LE BRET

What did you choose?

CYRANO

The simplest course of all. I decided to be admirable in everything!

LE BRET

(Shrugging)
If you say so. . . . But let me ask you something else.
What's the real reason for your hatred of Montfleury?
You can tell *me* the truth.

CYRANO

(Standing up)
That bloated old sot, with a belly so big he can't touch
his own navel, still considers himself a terror with the
ladies and gives them amorous looks with those froglike
eyes of his while he's bumbling his lines on the stage.
I've hated him since the day when I saw him look at . . .
It was like watching a slimy slug crawling on a flower!

LE BRET

(Astonished)
What's this? Do I understand you rightly? Is it possible that . . .

CYRANO

(With a bitter laugh)
That I'm in love? *(Changing to a grave tone)* Yes, it's
true.

LE BRET

May I ask with whom? You've never told me . . .

CYRANO

With whom I'm in love? Come now, think a moment:
this nose of mine, which precedes me by a quarter of an
hour wherever I go, forbids me ever to dream of being
loved by even an ugly woman. You ask me whom I love?
The answer should be clear to you! Whom else would I
love but the most beautiful woman in the world?

LE BRET

The most beautiful . . .

CYRANO

Of course! The most beautiful of all women! The most
captivating, the most intelligent . . . *(Dejectedly)* . . .
the blondest. . . .

LE BRET

For God's sake, tell me: who is she?

CYRANO

She's a mortal danger without meaning to be one; she's
exquisite without giving it a thought; she's a trap set by
nature, a rose in which love lies in ambush! Anyone who
has seen her smile has known perfection. She creates
grace without movement, and makes all divinity fit into
her slightest gesture. And neither Venus in her shell,
nor Diana striding in the great, blossoming forest, can
compare to her when she goes through the streets of
Paris in her sedan chair!

LE BRET

Now I believe I know! It *is* becoming clear!

CYRANO

It's perfectly transparent.

LE BRET

Your cousin, Magdeleine Robin?

CYRANO

Yes—Roxane.

LE BRET

Then you ought to be overjoyed! You love her? Tell her
so! You've covered yourself with glory in her eyes today.

CYRANO

Look at me and tell me what hope this protuberance
might leave me! I have no illusions. Sometimes, in the
blue shadows of evening, I give way to tender feelings.
I go into a garden, smelling the fragrance of spring with
my poor monstrous nose, and watch a man and a woman
strolling together in the moonlight. I think how much I,
too, would like to be walking arm in arm with a woman,
under the moon. I let myself be carried away, I forget
myself—and then I suddenly see the shadow of my pro-
file on the garden wall.

LE BRET

(Deeply moved)
My friend . . .

CYRANO

My friend, I have bad moments now and then, feeling
myself so ugly, all alone. . . .

LE BRET
(With concern, taking his hand)
Do you weep?

CYRANO
Oh, no, never! No, it would be grotesque if a tear ran
down this nose! As long as it's in my power to prevent
it, I'll never let the divine beauty of tears be sullied by
such gross ugliness. There's nothing more sublime than
tears, and I wouldn't want a single one of them to become an object of ridicule because of me.

LE BRET
Come, don't be sad! Love is only a game of chance!

CYRANO
(Shaking his head)
No! I love Cleopatra—do I look like a Caesar? I adore
Berenice—have I the appearance of a Titus?

LE BRET
But you're overlooking your courage, your wit! . . . Take
that girl who offered to give you dinner just now, for
example: you could see for yourself that she was far
from detesting you!

CYRANO
(Struck by this realization)
Yes, it's true!

LE BRET
Well, then? You see? And Roxane herself was pale as
she watched your duel. . . .

CYRANO
Pale?

LE BRET
You've already made a deep impression on her heart
and her mind. Don't be timid: speak to her, tell her,
so that . . .

CYRANO
So that she'll laugh in my face? No! That's the one thing
in the world that I fear!

THE DOORKEEPER
(Bringing in Roxane's DUENNA*)*
Sir, this lady would like to speak to you.

CYRANO
(Seeing the DUENNA*)*
My God! Her duenna!

Scene VI

Cyrano, Le Bret, the Duenna.

THE DUENNA
(With a deep bow)
My lady wishes me to ask her valiant cousin where she can see him in private.

CYRANO
(Thunderstruck)
See me?

THE DUENNA
(With another bow)
Yes. She has things to tell you.

CYRANO
Things to . . .

THE DUENNA
(Bowing again)
To tell you.

CYRANO
(Unsteady on his feet)
My God!

THE DUENNA
She will go to early Mass at the Saint-Roch church tomorrow morning.

CYRANO
(Clutching LE BRET *to steady himself)*
Ah, my God!

THE DUENNA

When she leaves the church, where can she go to talk
with you?

CYRANO

(Agitated)

Where? ... I ... My God! ... Where...

THE DUENNA

Well?

CYRANO

I'm trying to think!

THE DUENNA

Tell me.

CYRANO

At . . . at Ragueneau's shop . . . Ragueneau, the
pastry cook. . . .

THE DUENNA

Where is it?

CYRANO

It's ... it's on ... Oh, my God! ... It's on the ... the
Rue Saint-Honoré!

THE DUENNA

(Withdrawing)

Very well. At seven o'clock.

CYRANO

I'll be there.

(The DUENNA *leaves.)*

Scene VII

*Cyrano, Le Bret, then the Actors and Actresses, Cuigy,
Brissaille, Lignière, the Doorkeeper, the Violinists.*

CYRANO

(Falling into LE BRET's *arms)*

Me! She wants to see *me*!

LE BRET

I see your sadness has vanished!

CYRANO

Ah, for whatever reason, she knows I exist!

LE BRET

Please be calm.

CYRANO

No! I'm going to be frenzied and turbulent! I need a whole army to vanquish! I have ten hearts, twenty arms! It's no longer enough for me to cut down dwarfs . . . *(Shouts at the top of his lungs.)* . . . I need giants!
(For some time now, the ACTORS and ACTRESSES have been moving on the stage: the rehearsal is beginning. The VIOLINISTS have taken their places.)

A VOICE

(From the stage)
Quiet! We're rehearsing!

CYRANO

(Laughing)
And we're leaving!
(He goes upstage. Through the entrance of the theater come CUIGY, BRISSAILLE, and several OFFICERS holding up LIGNIÈRE, who is thoroughly drunk.)

CUIGY

Cyrano!

CYRANO

What is it?

CUIGY

We've brought a friend—much the worse for wine!

CYRANO

(Recognizing him)
Lignière! . . . What's happened to you?

CUIGY

He wants to see you.

BRISSAILLE

He can't go home.

CYRANO

Why not?

LIGNIÈRE
(In a thick voice, holding up a rumpled piece of paper)
This note warns me . . . hundred men against me . . . because of . . . of a song . . . great danger . . . Porte de Nesle . . . on my way home. . . . Will you let me . . . let me sleep under your roof tonight?

CYRANO

A hundred men, you say? You'll sleep at home tonight!

LIGNIÈRE
(Alarmed)
But . . .

CYRANO
(In a thunderous voice, pointing to the lighted lantern that the DOORKEEPER *has been holding while curiously listening to this scene)*
Take that lantern . . . (LIGNIÈRE *quickly obeys.*) . . . and walk! I'll cover you! *(To the* OFFICERS) And you, follow at a distance: you'll be witnesses!

CUIGY

But a hundred men! . . .

CYRANO

I need at least that many this evening!
(The ACTORS *and* ACTRESSES, *in their various costumes, have come down from the stage and approached the group.)*

LE BRET

But why should you risk your life . . .

CYRANO

Le Bret is grumbling again!

LE BRET

. . . for this drunkard?

CYRANO
(Patting LIGNIÈRE's *shoulder)*
Because this drunkard, this walking wine cask, once did
something admirable. When he saw the woman he loved
taking holy water as she was leaving church after Mass,
he hurried to the font, and even though he ordinarily
can't bear even the sight of water, drank it all!

AN ACTRESS
(Wearing a soubrette costume)
That was a lovely thing to do!

CYRANO
Yes, wasn't it?

THE ACTRESS
(To the others)
But why should there be a hundred men against one
poor poet?

CYRANO
Let's go! *(To the* OFFICERS*)* Gentlemen, when you see
me charge, don't come to my assistance, no matter how
great the danger!

ANOTHER ACTRESS
(Leaping down from the stage)
I want to go and watch!

CYRANO
Come along!

A THIRD ACTRESS
(Also leaping down from the stage, to an old ACTOR*)*
Are you coming, Cassandre?

CYRANO
Yes, come, all of you: the Doctor, Isabelle, Léandre—
everyone! You'll form a gay, charming troupe that will
add a note of Italian farce to this Spanish drama, and
you'll surround its solemnity with the merry sound of
your chatter, like jingling bells around a tambourine!

ALL THE WOMEN
(Jumping for joy)
Bravo!—Quick, a cloak! Where's my hood?

JODELET

We're off!

CYRANO

(To the VIOLINISTS*)*
You, gentlemen, will inspire us with your music as we march. *(The* VIOLINISTS *join the procession that is forming. Lighted candles are taken from the footlights and distributed. The scene takes on the aspect of a torchlight parade.)* Bravo! Officers, ladies in costume, and twenty paces in front . . . *(He takes up the station he has described.)* . . . I will walk alone, under the plume that glory herself has placed on my hat, with twice the pride of Scipio, and a nose three times as long! . . . Remember, now: no one is allowed to lift a finger to help me! . . . All ready? One, two, three! Doorkeeper, open the door! *(The* DOORKEEPER *opens both halves of the door, giving a glimpse of picturesque old Paris in the moonlight.)* Ah, Paris lies before us, dim and nebulous in the shadows, with moonlight flowing down the slopes of her roofs! An exquisite setting for the scene about to be performed! There, beneath the mist, the Seine quivers like a mysterious magic mirror. . . . And you will see what you will see!

ALL

To the Porte de Nesle!

CYRANO

(Standing on the threshold)
To the Porte de Nesle! *(Turns to the* SOUBRETTE.*)* You asked, mademoiselle, why a hundred men had been sent to attack one poet. *(Calmly, drawing his sword)* I'll tell you: it's because that poet is known to be a friend of mine. *(He goes out. The procession—*LIGNIÈRE *staggering in the lead, then the* ACTRESSES *on the arms of the* OFFICERS, *then the* ACTORS, *gamboling lightheartedly—moves forward into the night, to the sound of the violins, and in the dim glow of the candles.)*

CURTAIN

Act Two

❧

The Poets' Cookshop

*The large workroom of the shop of Ragueneau,
cookshop proprietor and pastry cook, at the corner
of the Rue Saint-Honoré and the Rue de l'Arbre-Sec.
The street, seen through the panes of the door in the
background, is gray in the first glow of dawn.*

*Downstage left, a counter surrounded by a
wrought-iron canopy from which geese, ducks, and
white peacocks are hanging. Large china vases hold
tall bouquets of common flowers, mainly sunflowers.
On the same side, farther back, an immense fireplace
in front of which, between the monstrous andirons,
each one supporting a small pot, roasts are dripping
into grease pans.*

*Downstage right, a door. Behind it, a staircase
leading up to a small room with a sloping ceiling,
seen through open shutters. A table has been set here,
and a small Flemish chandelier lighted; it is a room
for eating and drinking. A wooden gallery, extending
from the top of the stairs, seems to lead to other
such rooms.*

*In the middle of the workroom, various kinds of
game are hung from an iron hoop that can be lowered by a rope, forming a culinary chandelier. The
red glow of the ovens can be seen in the shadows
under the staircase. Copper pots and pans are gleam-*

*ing. Spits are turning. Pyramids of elaborate pastry,
hams hanging from the ceiling.*

*The morning rush has begun. Fat cooks, distraught
scullions, and small kitchen boys are jostling one another in a profusion of hats adorned with chicken
feathers or guinea-fowl wings. Mounds of brioches
and vast arrays of petits fours are being carried on
wicker trays and sheets of metal.*

*Some tables are covered with cakes and dishes.
Others, surrounded by chairs, are awaiting eaters and
drinkers. A smaller one in a corner is laden with
papers. Ragueneau is seated at it, writing, as the curtain rises.*

Scene I

*Ragueneau, Pastrycooks, then Lise; Ragueneau at the lit-
tle table, writing with an inspired air and counting on
his fingers.*

FIRST PASTRYCOOK
(Bringing a complicated construction on a tray)
Fruit in nougat!

SECOND PASTRYCOOK
(Bringing a dish)
Custard!

THIRD PASTRYCOOK
(Bringing a roast decorated with feathers)
Peacock!

FOURTH PASTRYCOOK
(Bringing a sheet of metal)
Cakes!

FIFTH PASTRYCOOK
(Bringing an earthenware pot)
Braised beef!
(RAGUENEAU stops writing and looks up.)

RAGUENEAU

The silver of dawn is already gleaming on the copper pots! Silence the god who sings within you, Ragueneau! The hour of the lute will come—it is now the hour of the oven! *(Stands up and speaks to a* COOK.*)* There's something lacking in this sauce.

THE COOK

What shall I do to it?

RAGUENEAU

Make it a little more lyrical.

THE COOK

(Puzzled)
What?

FIRST PASTRYCOOK

Tarts!

SECOND PASTRYCOOK

Pies!

RAGUENEAU
(In front of the fireplace)
Away, my Muse, lest your eyes be reddened by this mundane fire! *(To a* PASTRYCOOK, *pointing to some round loaves of bread)* The slit in these loaves is badly placed: the caesura should be in the middle, between the hemistitches! *(To another, pointing to an unfinished pie)* This palace of crust must have a roof. *(To a young* APPRENTICE *who is sitting on the floor, placing poultry on a spit)* Alternate the humble chickens with the stately turkeys on your spit, my son, as Malherbe* alternated long and short lines in his verse, and then turn stanzas of poultry above the fire!

ANOTHER APPRENTICE
(Bringing a tray covered with a cloth)
I've baked this in your honor, sir. I hope it will please you.
(He uncovers the tray, revealing a large pastry lyre.)

---

* François de Malherbe (1555–1628), a French poet who laid down precise and rigid rules for poetry.

RAGUENEAU

(Enraptured)
A lyre!

THE APPRENTICE

Made of pastry dough.

RAGUENEAU

(Deeply moved)
With candied fruit!

THE APPRENTICE

And I made the strings of sugar.

RAGUENEAU

(Giving him some money)
Here, go and drink to my health! *(Sees* LISE *coming in.)*
My wife! Quickly, go about your business—and hide that
money! *(To* LISE, *pointing to the lyre with embarrassment)* Isn't it beautiful?

LISE

It's ridiculous!
(She puts a pile of paper bags on the counter.)

RAGUENEAU

You've brought some paper bags? Good, thank you.
(Looks at them more closely.) Oh, no! My treasured
books! My friends' poetry! Desecrated, dismembered, to
make bags for pastry! You're as heartless as the Bacchantes who tore Orpheus to pieces!

LISE

(Sharply)
I have a right to make use of what your wretched scribblers leave here as their only payment!

RAGUENEAU

Don't insult those divine songbirds, you vulture!

LISE

You never called me such names before that rabble
began coming here!

RAGUENEAU

(Pointing to the bags)
How can you treat poetry with such disrespect?

LISE

I'll treat poetry however I please!

RAGUENEAU

I shudder to think of what you might do with prose!

Scene II

The same, with two Children who have just entered.

RAGUENEAU

What will you have, children?

FIRST CHILD

Three small pies, please.

RAGUENEAU

(Serving them)
Three small pies, hot and brown!

SECOND CHILD

Would you please wrap them?

RAGUENEAU

(Aside, with dismay)
Alas! One of my bags. . . . *(To the* CHILDREN*)* Very well.
*(Picks up a bag, and as he is about to put the pies into
it, reads from it.)* "Like Ulysses parting from
Penelope . . ." No, not this one! *(Sets the bag aside and
takes another. Reads.)* "Phoebus of the golden hair . . ."
Not this one! *(Puts it down.)*

LISE

(Impatiently)
Well, what are you waiting for?

RAGUENEAU

Nothing, nothing. . . . *(Takes a third bag and resigns
himself to using it.)* The sonnet to Phyllis! What a loss!

LISE

(Shrugging)
I'm glad you finally made up your mind, you poor
simpleton!

(She stands on a chair and begins putting dishes away on a shelf. As soon as her back is turned, RA-GUENEAU calls back the CHILDREN, who are already at the door.)

RAGUENEAU

Psst! . . . Children! . . . Give me back the sonnet to Phyllis and I'll give you six pies instead of three! *(The CHILDREN give him the bag, quickly take the pies, and leave. He smooths the rumpled bag and begins reading.)* "Phyllis . . ." A spot of butter on that lovely name! "Phyllis . . ."
    (CYRANO enters abruptly.)

Scene III

Ragueneau, Lise, Cyrano, then the Musketeer.

CYRANO

What time is it?

RAGUENEAU

   (Bowing to him)
Six o'clock.

CYRANO

   (With great emotion)
One more hour!
   (He begins pacing the floor.)

RAGUENEAU

   (Following him)
Congratulations!

CYRANO

For what?

RAGUENEAU

I saw your duel!

CYRANO

Which one?

RAGUENEAU

At the Hôtel de Bourgogne!

CYRANO

(Disdainfully)
Oh, that one. . . .

RAGUENEAU

(Admiringly)
A duel in verse!

LISE

He talks about nothing else!

CYRANO

I'm glad to hear it.

RAGUENEAU

(Lunging with a spit that he has picked up)
"When I end the refrain, I draw blood! . . . When I end
the refrain, I draw blood!" Magnificent! *(With growing
enthusiasm)* "When I end the refrain . . ."

CYRANO

What time is it, Ragueneau?

RAGUENEAU

*(Looking at the clock while holding the position of
the lunge he has just made)*
Five past six. ". . . I draw blood!" *(Stands up straight.)*
Ah, what a ballade!

LISE

(To CYRANO, *who has absentmindedly shaken her
hand while passing by her counter)*
Your hand is wounded!

CYRANO

It's nothing, just a small gash.

RAGUENEAU

Have you been doing something dangerous?

CYRANO

No, I've been in no danger.

LISE
(Shaking her finger at him)
I believe you're telling a lie!

CYRANO

Why? Was my nose twitching? If so, it must have been an enormous lie! *(Changing his tone)* I'm waiting for someone here. If I don't wait in vain, I want you to leave us alone together.

RAGUENEAU

I can't do that: my poets will soon be here.

LISE

(Sarcastically)
For their first meal!

CYRANO

You will take them away when I give you a signal. . . . What time is it?

RAGUENEAU

Ten past six.

CYRANO
(Nervously sitting down at RAGUENEAU'*s table and taking a sheet of paper)*
May I have a pen?

RAGUENEAU
(Giving him the pen he has been carrying behind his ear)
Here, take my swan's feather!
(A MUSKETEER *with a superb mustache enters.)*

THE MUSKETEER
(In a stentorian voice)
Greetings!
*(*LISE *hurries toward him.)*

CYRANO
(Looking around)
Who's that?

RAGUENEAU

A friend of my wife's. A mighty warrior—according to what he says! He . . .

CYRANO

(Taking his pen again and waving RAGUENEAU *away)*
Never mind. *(To himself)* Write a note . . . fold it . . .
give it to her . . . run away. . . . *(Throws down the pen.)*
Coward! You don't have the courage to say one word
to her! *(To* RAGUENEAU*)* What time is it?

RAGUENEAU

Quarter past six.

CYRANO

(To himself)
I'm afraid to speak a single one of all the words I have
in here. *(Strikes his chest.)* But writing is a different
matter. . . . *(Takes his pen again.)* I'll now put down on
paper the love letter that I've already written within myself a hundred times. I have only to look into my soul
and copy the words inscribed in it.
*(He begins writing. Through the glass of the door,
thin figures are seen moving hesitantly.)*

Scene IV

*Ragueneau, Lise, the Musketeer, Cyrano, writing at the
little table, the Poets, dressed in black, with sagging,
muddy stockings.*

LISE

(Entering, to RAGUENEAU*)*
Here come your mud-spattered poets!

FIRST POET

(Entering, to RAGUENEAU*)*
Colleague!

SECOND POET

(Taking RAGUENEAU'S *hand)*
Dear colleague!

THIRD POET

Eagle of pastry cooks! *(Sniffs.)* What a fragrant nest you have!

FOURTH POET

O culinary god!

FIFTH POET

Apollo of the kitchen!

RAGUENEAU
(Surrounded, embraced, shaken)
They always make me feel at ease as soon as they come in!

FIRST POET

We were delayed by a crowd gathered at the Porte de Nesle.

SECOND POET

Eight bandits had been felled by swordplay and lay bleeding on the pavement!

CYRANO
(Briefly looking up)
Eight? I thought there were only seven.
(Resumes writing his letter.)

RAGUENEAU
(To CYRANO)
Do you know the hero of that combat?

CYRANO
(Casually)
No.

LISE
(To the MUSKETEER)
And you?

THE MUSKETEER
(Twirling his mustache)
Perhaps!

CYRANO

(Writing)
"I love you. . . ."
(He is heard murmuring from time to time.)

FIRST POET

We were told that one man had routed a whole band
of assassins!

SECOND POET

There were pikes and clubs strewn all over the ground!

CYRANO

(Writing)
"Your eyes . . ."

THIRD POET

And hats were found as far away as the Quai des
Orfèvres!

FIRST POET

The man who could do a thing like that . . .

CYRANO

(Writing)
"Your lips . . ."

FIRST POET

. . . must have been some sort of ferocious giant!

CYRANO

(Writing)
". . . and I become faint with fear each time I see you."

SECOND POET

(Snatching a cake)
What have you been writing, Ragueneau?

CYRANO

(Writing)
"Your faithful worshiper . . ." *(He stops as he is about
to sign his name, stands up, and puts the letter in his
doublet.)* No need to sign it, since I'll give it to her
myself.

RAGUENEAU

(To the SECOND POET)
I've written a recipe in verse.

THIRD POET
(Sitting down next to a tray of cream puffs)
Let's hear it!

FOURTH POET
(Looking at a brioche that he has picked up)
This brioche has put its hat on crooked.
(Bites off the top of it.)

FIRST POET
This gingerbread gazes at a hungry poet with its almond
eyes and warm, inviting smile!
(Takes the piece of gingerbread.)

SECOND POET
(To RAGUENEAU*)*
We're listening.

THIRD POET
(Lightly squeezing a cream puff between his fingers)
See how this cream puff drools with delight!

SECOND POET
(Biting into the pastry lyre)
For the first time, the Lyre gives me sustenance!

RAGUENEAU
*(Clears his throat, straightens his hat, strikes a pose,
and prepares to recite.)*
A recipe in verse . . .

SECOND POET
(To the first, nudging him)
Are you having breakfast?

FIRST POET
(To the second)
Yes, and you're eating dinner!

RAGUENEAU
"How to Make Almond Tarts"

Beat some eggs till they are foamy;
Mix with tangy citron juice;
Then fold in sweet milk of almonds.
Line your pans with pastry dough,
Slowly pour your foam to fill them;

Let them bake till golden brown.
Now remove them from the oven:
Luscious, dainty almond tarts!

THE POETS
(With their mouths full)
Exquisite! Delightful!

A POET
(Choking)
Omph!
(They go upstage, still eating. CYRANO, *who has been watching, approaches* RAGUENEAU.*)*

CYRANO
Haven't you ever noticed how they stuff themselves while they listen to your verse?

RAGUENEAU
(In a low voice, with a smile)
Of course, but I never let them know it, because I don't want to embarrass them. I take double pleasure in reciting my compositions like that: I satisfy my little weakness, and at the same time I feed brother poets who would otherwise go hungry.

CYRANO
(Affectionately clapping him on the shoulder)
You're a fine fellow, Ragueneau! *(*RAGUENEAU *goes to rejoin his friends.* CYRANO *watches him walk away, then speaks rather brusquely.)* Lise! *(*LISE, *in tender conversation with the* MUSKETEER, *starts, and then comes toward* CYRANO.*)* Is that musketeer laying siege to you?

LISE
(Offended)
If a man tries to attack my virtue, I stop him with a single withering look.

CYRANO
"Withering" is hardly the word to describe the look you were giving your friend just now.

LISE
(Taken aback)
But . . .

CYRANO

(Bluntly)

I like Ragueneau. That's why I won't allow anyone to make him play the ridiculous part of a deceived husband.

LISE

But . . .

CYRANO

(Raising his voice in order to be heard by the MUSKETEER*)*

A word to the wise. . . .

(He bows to the MUSKETEER *and goes to take up his observation post at the door in the background, after looking at the clock.)*

LISE

(To the MUSKETEER, *who has merely returned* CYRANO's *bow in silence)*

Well? Aren't you going to say anything? I'm surprised you haven't already thrown your answer against his nose!

THE MUSKETEER

His nose? Oh, his nose! . . .

(He quickly walks away. LISE *follows him.)*

CYRANO

(From the door in the background, motioning RA-GUENEAU *to take the* POETS *away)*

Psst! . . .

RAGUENEAU

(Showing the POETS *the door on the right)*

Come this way, gentlemen, we'll be much more comfortable . . .

CYRANO

(Impatiently)

Psst! psst!

RAGUENEAU

(Leading them away)

. . . for reading poetry.

FIRST POET
(Despairingly, with his mouth full)
But what about the cakes?

SECOND POET
Let's take them with us!
(They all go out behind RAGUENEAU, *in procession, after having snatched up several trays of pastry.)*

Scene V

Cyrano, Roxane, the Duenna.

CYRANO
I'll give her my letter if I feel that there's the slightest hope! *(*ROXANE, *masked, appears behind the glass of the door, followed by the* DUENNA. *He throws open the door.)* Come in! *(Takes the* DUENNA *aside.)* May I have a word with you?

THE DUENNA
Have several, if you like.

CYRANO
Are you fond of pastry?

THE DUENNA
I'm sinfully fond of it!

CYRANO
(Quickly taking some of the paper bags on the counter)
Good. Here are two sonnets by Monsieur Benserade . . .

THE DUENNA
(Disappointed)
Oh. . . .

CYRANO
. . . which I will fill with custard tarts for you.
(The DUENNA's *face brightens.)*

THE DUENNA
Ah!

CYRANO

Do you like cream puffs?

THE DUENNA

(With dignity)
I hold them in high regard.

CYRANO

Here are six of them for you, in a poem by Saint-Amant.
And in this verse by Chapelain* I'll place a piece of
butter cake. You really like pastry, do you?

THE DUENNA

I adore it!

CYRANO

(Loading her arms with filled bags)
Then I'm sure you'll enjoy going out and eating all this
in the street.

THE DUENNA

But . . .

CYRANO

(Pushing her outside)
And please don't come back until you've finished.
(He closes the door, approaches ROXANE, *and stops
at a respectful distance with his hat in his hand.)*

Scene VI

Cyrano, Roxane, the Duenna for a moment.

CYRANO

May this day be blessed above all others: the day when
you ceased to forget my existence and came here to tell
me . . . to tell me? . . .

ROXANE

(Who has taken off her mask)
First let me thank you for humbling that arrogant fop

* Marc-Antoine de Gérard, Sieur de Saint-Amant (1594–1661),
and Jean Chapelain (1595–1674): poets who were among the original members of the French Academy.

with your sword yesterday, because he's the man whom a certain great lord, infatuated with me . . .

CYRANO

De Guiche?

ROXANE

(Lowering her eyes)

. . . was trying to impose on me as . . . as a husband. . . .

CYRANO

A husband only for the sake of form? *(Bows.)* I'm happy to know that I fought not for my ugly nose, but for your beautiful eyes.

ROXANE

And then, I wanted to tell you . . . But before I make my confession, give me time to see you again as I did in the past, when I thought of you almost as my brother. We used to play together in the park, beside the lake. . . .

CYRANO

Yes. . . . You came to Bergerac every summer.

ROXANE

You used a reed for a sword in those days!

CYRANO

And you used corn silk to make hair for your dolls.

ROXANE

We played all sorts of games.

CYRANO

And ate blackberries before they were ripe.

ROXANE

You always did whatever I wanted!

CYRANO

You weren't yet known as Roxane. In short skirts, you were still called Magdeleine.

ROXANE

Was I pretty then?

CYRANO

You weren't ugly.

ROXANE

Sometimes you came to me with your hand bleeding
from some accident and I acted as if I were your mother,
trying to make my voice stern. *(Takes his hand.)* "What's
this?" I'd say. "Have you hurt yourself again?" *(Looks
at his hand.)* Oh! Even now! You've done it again! *(CY-
RANO tries to withdraw his hand.)* No! Let me see!
You're still hurting yourself, at your age! How did you
do it this time?

CYRANO

I was playing again—at the Porte de Nesle.

ROXANE

*(Sits down at a table and wets her handkerchief in a
glass of water.)*
Give me that hand!

CYRANO

(Also sits down.)
You still mother me!

ROXANE

While I wash away this blood, I want you to describe
what happened. How many were there against you?

CYRANO

Oh, not quite a hundred.

ROXANE

Tell me about it!

CYRANO

No, never mind. Tell me what you couldn't bring yourself to say just now.

ROXANE

(Without letting go of his hand)
Yes, I can say it now that the past has returned to en-
courage me. Here it is. I'm in love with someone.

CYRANO

Ah! . . .

ROXANE

Someone who doesn't know.

CYRANO

Ah! . . .

ROXANE

Not yet.

CYRANO

Ah! . . .

ROXANE

But he *will* know soon.

CYRANO

Ah! . . .

ROXANE

He's a poor man who till now has loved me timidly, from a distance, without daring to say anything.

CYRANO

Ah! . . .

ROXANE

Let me keep your hand, it feels feverish. . . . But I've seen a confession of love trembling on his lips.

CYRANO

Ah! . . .

ROXANE

(Bandaging his hand with her handkerchief)
And it so happens, cousin, that he's a member of your regiment.

CYRANO

Ah! . . .

ROXANE

(Smiling)
In fact, he's a Cadet in your company!

CYRANO

Ah! . . .

ROXANE

His face shines with wit and intelligence. He's proud, noble, young, fearless, handsome. . . .

CYRANO
(Standing up, with a stricken expression)
Handsome!

ROXANE

What is it? What's the matter?

CYRANO

Nothing. . . . It's . . . it's . . . *(Shows her his hand, with a smile.)* It's only a twinge of pain from this little scratch.

ROXANE

Well, I love him, even though I've never seen him any-where but in the theater.

CYRANO

You've never spoken to each other?

ROXANE

Only with our eyes.

CYRANO

Then how do you know he loves you?

ROXANE

Under the linden trees of the Place Royale, people gossip. . . . Talkative acquaintances have told me. . . .

CYRANO

You say he's a Cadet?

ROXANE

Yes, in the Guards.

CYRANO

His name?

ROXANE

Baron Christian de Neuvillette.

CYRANO

Neuvillette? There's no Cadet by that name.

ROXANE

There is now. He began serving only this morning, under Captain Carbon de Castel-Jaloux.

CYRANO

You've lost your heart so quickly! But, my poor girl . . .

THE DUENNA
(Opening the door in the background)
I've eaten all the pastry, Monsieur de Bergerac!

CYRANO

Then read the poetry on the bags! *(The* DUENNA *disappears.)* My poor girl, you're so fond of fine words and gracious wit—what if he should prove to be an uncultured savage?

ROXANE

Impossible. He has the hair of one of d'Urfé's* heroes!

CYRANO

His speech may be as crude as his hair is elegant.

ROXANE

No, there's delicacy in everything he says. I feel it!

CYRANO

Yes, all words are delicate when they come from lips adorned with a shapely mustache. . . . But what if he's a fool?

ROXANE
(Stamping her foot)
Then I'll die! There, are you satisfied?

CYRANO
(After a time)
You brought me here to tell me this? I confess I don't quite understand why.

ROXANE

It's because someone terrified me yesterday by telling

* Honoré d'Urfé (1567–1625), French novelist whose heroes were taken as paragons of chivalrous manhood in the seventeenth century.

me that most of you in your company are Gascons,
and . . .

CYRANO

And that we always provoke a duel with any newcomer
who gains the favor of being admitted among us without
being a Gascon? Is that what you were told?

ROXANE

Yes. You can imagine how I trembled for him when I
heard it!

CYRANO

(Aside)
And with good reason!

ROXANE

But when I saw you yesterday, great and invincible, punishing that scoundrel and holding all those brutes at bay,
I said to myself, "Everyone fears him. If he were willing to . . ."

CYRANO

Very well, I'll protect your little baron.

ROXANE

Oh, I knew you would! I've always had such tender af-
fection for you. . . .

CYRANO

Yes, yes.

ROXANE

You'll be his friend?

CYRANO

I will.

ROXANE

And he'll never have a duel?

CYRANO

No. I promise.

ROXANE

I knew I was right to like you so much! And now I must
go. *(Quickly puts on her mask and speaks distractedly.)*
But you haven't told me about your battle last night. It

must have been incredible! . . . Tell him to write to me.
(Throws him a kiss.) Oh, I love you!

CYRANO

Yes, yes.

ROXANE

A hundred men against you? Well, good-by. You're my
best friend!

CYRANO

Yes, yes.

ROXANE

Tell him to write! . . . A hundred men! You'll tell me
about it some other time; I can't stay now. A hundred
men! What courage!

CYRANO

(Bowing to her)
Oh, I've done better since then.
*(She leaves. He remains motionless, looking down at
the floor. A silence, then the door opens and RA-
GUENEAU puts in his head.)*

Scene VII

*Cyrano, Ragueneau, the Poets, Carbon de Castel-Jaloux,
the Cadets, the Crowd, etc., then De Guiche.*

RAGUENEAU

May we come back in?

CYRANO

(Without moving)
Yes.
*(RAGUENEAU signals to his friends and they come in.
At the same time CARBON DE CASTEL-JALOUX, dressed
as a Captain of the Guards, appears at the door in
the background and makes broad gestures when he
sees CYRANO.)*

CARBON

Here he is!

CYRANO
(Looking up)
Captain!

CARBON
(Exultant)
Our hero! We know all about it! Thirty of my Cadets
are here!

CYRANO
(Stepping back)
But . . .

CARBON
(Trying to lead him out)
Come! They want to see you!

CYRANO
No!

CARBON
They're drinking in the tavern across the street, the
Croix du Trahoir.

CYRANO
I . . .

CARBON
*(Goes back to the doorway and shouts through it in
a thunderous voice.)*
Our hero won't come! He's in a bad mood!

A VOICE
(From outside)
Sandious!*
*(Tumult outside, with a clatter of swords
approaching)*

CARBON
(Rubbing his hands together)
Here they come!

THE CADETS
(Entering)
Mille dioux!—Capdedious!—Mordious!—Pocapdedious!

* A Gascon exclamation, as are *mille dioux, capdedious, mordious,* and *pocapdedious,* below.

RAGUENEAU

(Stepping back in alarm)

Gentlemen, your language tells me that you're all from Gascony!

THE CADETS

Yes, all of us!

A CADET

(To CYRANO*)*

Bravo!

CYRANO

(Nodding)

Baron.

SECOND CADET

(Shaking CYRANO'S *hands)*

Hurrah!

CYRANO

Baron.

THIRD CADET

Let me embrace you!

CYRANO

Baron.

SEVERAL CADETS

Let's all embrace him!

CYRANO

(Not knowing which one to answer)

Baron . . . Baron . . . please. . . .

RAGUENEAU

Are you all barons, gentlemen?

THE CADETS

All?

RAGUENEAU

Yes.

FIRST CADET

We could build a tower with our baronial coronets!

LE BRET

(Entering and hurrying to CYRANO)

Everyone wants to see you! There's a wild crowd led by
those who were with you last night. . . .

CYRANO

(Alarmed)

You didn't tell them I was here, did you?

LE BRET

(Rubbing his hands together)

Of course I did!

A BURGHER

(Entering, followed by a group)

Sir, all the fashionable people in Paris are coming here!
*(Outside, the street is filled with people. Sedan chairs
and carriages are stopping.)*

LE BRET

(Softly, smiling at CYRANO)

Have you seen Roxane?

CYRANO

(Sharply)

Quiet!

THE CROWD

(Shouting from outside)

Cyrano!
(A throng bursts into the shop. Jostling. Cheers.)

RAGUENEAU

(Standing on a table)

They're invading my shop! They're breaking everything!
It's magnificent!

PEOPLE

(Around CYRANO)

My friend!—My friend!

CYRANO

I didn't have so many friends yesterday!

LE BRET

(Delighted)

What a triumph!

A YOUNG MARQUIS
(Rushing toward CYRANO *with hands outstretched)*
If you only knew, my dear Cyrano . . .

CYRANO

Your dear Cyrano? How can I have endeared myself to
you when I've never seen you before?

ANOTHER MARQUIS
Sir, I'd like to introduce you to some ladies who are
outside in my carriage.

CYRANO

(Coldly)
And who will introduce me to *you*?

LE BRET

(Surprised)
What's the matter with you?

CYRANO

Quiet!

A MAN OF LETTERS
(With a writing case)
Would you give me a few details of . . .

CYRANO

No.

LE BRET

(Nudging him)
That's Théophraste Renaudot!*

CYRANO

Well, what of it?

LE BRET

He's the inventor of the gazette, that printed sheet which
tells so many things. They say it's an idea with a great
future.

---

* Théophraste Renaudot (1586–1653) founded the first French
newspaper in 1631, originally titled *La Gazette,* then *La Gazette de
France.* In seventeenth-century France, "gazette" was the generic
word for "newspaper."

A POET

(Coming forward)

Sir . . .

CYRANO

Another one!

THE POET

I want to compose a pentacrostic on your name. . . .

A MAN

(Also coming forward)

Sir . . .

CYRANO

Enough!

(Movement, then the disorder of the crowd begins to subside. DE GUICHE *enters, escorted by* OFFICERS, *then* CUIGY, BRISSAILLE, *and the* OFFICERS *who left with* CYRANO *at the end of Act I.* CUIGY *hurries to* CYRANO.)

CUIGY

(To CYRANO*)*

Monsieur de Guiche . . . *(Murmurs. Everyone stands aside.)* . . . has come with a message from Marshal de Gassion!

DE GUICHE

(Bowing to CYRANO*)*

The Marshal has just learned of your latest exploit and wishes me to express his admiration to you.

THE CROWD

Bravo!

CYRANO

(Bowing)

The Marshal is an authority on daring deeds.

DE GUICHE

He would never have believed it if these gentlemen hadn't sworn to have seen it.

CUIGY

With our own eyes!

LE BRET
(Aside, to CYRANO, *who appears to be distracted)*
Aren't you going to . . .

CYRANO

Quiet!

LE BRET
You seem to be suffering!

CYRANO
(Starting, then quickly drawing himself erect)
In front of all these people? *(His mustache bristles; he
throws out his chest.)* I, suffering? You'll see!

DE GUICHE
(To whom CUIGY *has been whispering)*
Your career is already rich in noble exploits. You serve
with those wild Gascons, don't you?

CYRANO
Yes, I'm a Cadet in the Guards.

A CADET
(With fierce pride)
He's one of us!

DE GUICHE
(Looking at the Gascons grouped behind CYRANO)
Ah! Then all these haughty-looking gentlemen are the
famous . . .

CARBON

Cyrano!

CYRANO

Yes, Captain?

CARBON
Since all the men of my company are here, please introduce them to the Count.

CYRANO
(Taking two steps toward DE GUICHE *and pointing to
the* CADETS)
These are the stouthearted Gascon Cadets
Of Carbon de Castel Jaloux;

They fight over trifles and shamelessly lie;
These are the stouthearted Gascon Cadets!
Their knowledge of heraldry can't be surpassed;
No plowman can claim nobler birth;
These are the stouthearted Gascon Cadets
Of Carbon de Castel-Jaloux.

Keen-eyed as eagles and fiercer than wolves,
With the elegant grace of a cat,
They sweep all before them, wherever they go,
Keen-eyed as eagles and fiercer than wolves,
Wearing their battered old hats jauntily,
With feathers to cover the holes,
Keen-eyed as eagles and fiercer than wolves,
With the elegant grace of a cat.

Skull-Breaker, Cutthroat, Gut-Sticker, and Slash
Are the most peaceful nicknames they bear;
A passion for glory obsesses them all,
Skull-Breaker, Cutthroat, Gut-Sticker, and Slash
Wherever there's brawling, you'll find them on hand,
Each doing his share, and much more;
Skull-Breaker, Cutthroat, Gut-Sticker, and Slash
Are the most peaceful nicknames they bear.

These are the stouthearted Gascon Cadets
Who cuckold young husbands and old;
Adorable ladies, your virtue is doomed,
These are the stouthearted Gascon Cadets!
Your jealous defenders may grumble and scowl,
They're powerless to alter their fate;
These are the stouthearted Gascon Cadets
Who cuckold young husbands and old.

DE GUICHE
(Casually seated in an armchair that RAGUENEAU *has
quickly brought for him)*
Poets are a fashionable luxury these days. Would you
like to become one of my followers?

CYRANO
No, sir, I prefer to follow no one.

DE GUICHE
My uncle, Cardinal Richelieu, was amused by your dash-

ing combat yesterday. I'm willing to help you with him, if you like.

LE BRET

(Dazzled)
My God!

DE GUICHE

You've written a play, I believe. . . .

LE BRET

(Aside, to CYRANO*)*
Your *Agrippine** will soon be performed, my friend!

DE GUICHE

Take it to him.

CYRANO

(Tempted and rather pleased)
Really, I . . .

DE GUICHE

He knows a great deal about the theater. He'll rewrite a few lines. . . .

CYRANO

(Whose face has immediately darkened)
Impossible, sir; my blood curdles at the thought of having a single comma changed.

DE GUICHE

But when a piece of writing pleases him, he pays very well for it.

CYRANO

He couldn't pay as well as I do. When I write something that I like, I reward the author by reciting it to myself.

DE GUICHE

You're a proud man.

CYRANO

Have you noticed that?
(A CADET *enters, holding his sword aloft to display*

---

* *La Mort d'Agrippine* is a play written by the real Cyrano.

the hats that are spitted on it. They are all shabby and misshapen, with bedraggled plumes.)

THE CADET

Look, Cyrano, at the strange feathered game we took in the street this morning! The men you routed seem to have run away too fast for their hats to follow them!

CARBON

The spoils of war!

EVERYONE

(Laughing)
Ha! ha! ha!

CUIGY

The man who hired those cowardly brutes must be in a rage today!

BRISSAILLE

Do you know who did it?

DE GUICHE

I did. *(The laughter ceases.)* I hired them for a task that one doesn't do oneself: punishing a drunken rhymester.
(Uncomfortable silence)

THE CADET

(Aside, to CYRANO, *showing him the hats)*
What shall we do with these? They're greasy—shall we make them into a stew?
(CYRANO takes the sword on which the hats are spitted and lowers it in a gesture of homage to DE GUICHE, *making them all slide off onto the floor at his feet.)*

CYRANO

Sir, would you like to take these back to your friends?

DE GUICHE

(In a peremptory tone, standing up)
Bring my sedan chair immediately. I'm leaving. *(To* CYRANO, *violently)* You, sir! . . .

A VOICE

(Shouting, from outside)
Porters! Bring Monsieur de Guiche's chair!

DE GUICHE
(With a smile, having regained his self-control)
Have you read *Don Quixote*?

CYRANO
Yes, I have, and I take off my hat to you in the name
of that scatterbrained hero.

DE GUICHE
You would do well to meditate . . .

A PORTER
(Appearing in the background)
The sedan chair is here.

DE GUICHE
. . . on the chapter concerning windmills.

CYRANO
(Bowing)
Chapter Thirteen.

DE GUICHE
Because when one attacks them . . .

CYRANO
Do you mean to say that I attack people who veer with
every change of wind?

DE GUICHE
When one attacks them, their great arms often hurl one
down into the mud!

CYRANO
Or up into the stars!
*(DE GUICHE leaves. He is seen getting into his sedan
chair. The OFFICERS walk away, whispering to one
another. LE BRET accompanies them to the door. The
CROWD leaves.)*

Scene VIII

*Cyrano, Le Bret, the Cadets, who are seated at tables to
left and right and are being served food and drink.*

CYRANO
(Mockingly bowing to those who are leaving without daring to bid him good-by)
Gentlemen. . . . Gentlemen. . . . Gentlemen. . . .

LE BRET
(Coming back from the door and throwing up his arms in despair)
This time you've outdone yourself!

CYRANO
Must I listen to your complaining again?

LE BRET
You shatter every opportunity that comes your way! You'll have to admit that you go too far!

CYRANO
Yes, I go too far.

LE BRET
(Triumphantly)
You *do* admit it!

CYRANO
But for the sake of principle, and to set an example, too, I feel that it's good to go too far in that direction.

LE BRET
If you would only soften your haughty spirit a little, fortune and glory would . . .

CYRANO
But what would I have to do? Cover myself with the protection of some powerful patron? Imitate the ivy that licks the bark of a tall tree while entwining itself around its trunk, and make my way upward by guile, rather than climbing by my own strength? No, thank you. Dedicate poems to financiers, as so many others do? Change myself into a buffoon in the hope of seeing a minister give me a condescending smile? No, thank you. Swallow insults every day? Crawl till the skin of my belly is rubbed raw? Dirty my knees and make my spine as limber as an eel's? No, thank you. Develop the art of sitting on both sides of a fence at once? Pay for an ounce of favor with a ton of flattery? No, thank you. Use women as

stepping-stones? Make headway in the sea of life with madrigals for oars and the sighs of old ladies for the wind in my sails? No, thank you. Have poetry published at my own expense? No, thank you. Attend councils held in taverns by imbeciles, trying to win the honor of being chosen as their pope? No, thank you. Work to make a name for myself with one sonnet, instead of writing others? No, thank you. See talent only in nonentities? Be terrified of the gazettes, and constantly be thinking, "Oh, if only the *Mercure François* will say a kind word about me?" No, thank you. Be always scheming and afraid of schemes? Like paying visits better than writing poetry? Make humble requests? Seek introductions to useful people? No, thank you! No! No! I prefer to lead a different kind of life. I sing, dream, laugh, and go where I please, alone and free. My eyes see clearly and my voice is strong. I'm quarrelsome or benign as it suits my pleasure, always ready to fight a duel or write a poem at the drop of a hat. I dream of flying to the moon but give no thought to fame or fortune. I write only what comes out of myself, and I make it my modest rule to be satisfied with whatever flowers, fruit, or even leaves I gather, as long as they're from my own garden. Then if I should happen to gain some small success I'm not obliged to render any of it unto Caesar. In short, I scorn to be like parasitic ivy, even though I'm not an oak. I may not rise very high, but I'll climb alone!

LE BRET

Be alone if you like, but why have everyone against you? How the devil did you acquire that appalling mania for making enemies wherever you go?

CYRANO

I acquired it by watching others make multitudes of friends and laugh at them behind their backs! I like to exchange as few greetings as possible when I go out, and I'm always glad to add another enemy to my list.

LE BRET

Sheer perversity!

CYRANO

Let's call it my vice. It pleases me to displease. I love

to be hated. If you only knew how stimulating it is to
be under the murderous fire of hostile eyes, and how
amusing it is to watch faces turn venomous with envy or
sweaty with fear! The soft friendship that surrounds others is like one of those loose, floating Italian collars that
leave your neck free to bend in all directions: you're
more comfortable, but your head is less erect. But the
hatred that presses in upon me is like a starched Spanish
ruff whose stiffness forces me to hold my head high.
Each new enemy is a pleat that constrains me still more,
yet adds to my splendor, because hatred is both a yoke
and a halo of glory!

LE BRET
(After a silence, passing his arm under CYRANO's)
Proclaim your pride and bitterness loudly to the world,
but to me speak softly and tell me simply that she
doesn't love you.

CYRANO
(Sharply)
Stop! Enough!
*(*CHRISTIAN *has entered some time earlier and min-
gled with the* CADETS, *who have not spoken to him.
He has finally sat down alone at a small table where*
LISE *is now serving him.)*

Scene IX

Cyrano, Le Bret, the Cadets, Christian de Neuvillette.

A CADET
(Seated at a table upstage, with a glass in his hand)
Cyrano! *(*CYRANO *looks around.)* Will you tell us your
story now?

CYRANO
Not now. A little later.
(He and LE BRET *walk upstage, arm in arm, talking
quietly together.)*

THE CADET
(Standing up and coming downstage)
The story of Cyrano's combat will be the best lesson . . .
(Stops at CHRISTIAN's *table.)* . . . for this timid apprentice.

CHRISTIAN
(Looking up)
Apprentice?

ANOTHER CADET
Yes, you sickly northerner.

CHRISTIAN
Sickly?

FIRST CADET
(Banteringly)
Monsieur de Neuvillette, it's time for you to learn something. There's a certain object that we all avoid naming as scrupulously as we would refrain from mentioning rope in the house of a man whose father had been hanged.

CHRISTIAN
What is it?

THIRD CADET
(With majestic authority)
Look at me! *(Puts his finger to his nose three times, mysteriously.)* Do you understand?

CHRISTIAN
I think so. You must mean . . .

FOURTH CADET
Sh! You must never speak that word! *(Points to* CYRANO, *who is still talking upstage with* LE BRET.*)* If you do, you'll have *him* to deal with!

FIFTH CADET
(Who has silently sat down on CHRISTIAN's *table while his head was turned toward the others)*
He's already killed two men because they had nasal voices!

SIXTH CADET
(In a hollow tone, standing up after having crawled under the table)
The slightest allusion to that protuberance brings an untimely death!

SEVENTH CADET
(Putting his hand on CHRISTIAN's *shoulder)*
One word is enough! Even a gesture! If you take out your handkerchief, you've taken out your shroud!
(Silence. The CADETS *are all around* CHRISTIAN, *looking at him with their arms folded. He stands up and goes to* CARBON DE CASTEL-JALOUX, *who is talking with an* OFFICER *and seems unaware of what has been taking place.)*

CHRISTIAN
Captain!

CARBON
(Turning around and looking him up and down)
Yes?

CHRISTIAN
What should one do when southerners become too boastful?

CARBON
Prove to them that a northerner can be courageous.
(Turns his back on CHRISTIAN.)

CHRISTIAN
Thank you.

FIRST CADET
(To CYRANO)
Now tell us your story!

ALL
Your story!

CYRANO
(Comes toward them.)
My story? . . . *(They all draw up their stools and group themselves around him, straining their necks forward.* CHRISTIAN *has straddled a chair.)* Well, I was walking

alone to meet them. The moon was gleaming like a big silver watch in the sky when suddenly some heavenly hand slipped it into a pocket of clouds. The sky was black as pitch and there were no lights in the street. I couldn't see . . .

CHRISTIAN

Beyond the end of your nose.
(Silence. The CADETS *all stand up slowly, looking at* CYRANO *in terror. He has stopped short, dumb-founded. Several moments of tense waiting go by before he finally speaks.)*

CYRANO

Who is this man?

A CADET

(In a low voice)
He came to us only this morning.

CYRANO

(Taking a step toward CHRISTIAN*)*
This morning?

CARBON

(In a low voice)
His name is Baron de Neuvil—

CYRANO

(Quickly, stopping)
Oh! *(His face takes on an expression of shock, then anger, and he makes a movement as though to attack* CHRISTIAN.*)* I . . . *(He controls himself and speaks dully.)* Very well. . . . As I was saying . . . *(With a burst of rage in his voice) Mordious! (Continues in a natural tone.)* It was so dark that I couldn't see anything. *(The* CADETS *are amazed. They sit down again, staring at him.)* I walked on, thinking that for the sake of a poor drunkard I was about to anger some powerful nobleman who would surely . . .

CHRISTIAN

Resent your nosiness.
(The CADETS *all stand up again.* CHRISTIAN *tilts his chair.)*

CYRANO

(Choking)

. . . who would surely bear a grudge against me, and
that I was rashly putting . . .

CHRISTIAN

Your nose into . . .

CYRANO

. . . myself into a bad situation, because that nobleman
might . . .

CHRISTIAN

Look down his nose at you.

CYRANO

(Wiping sweat from his forehead)

. . . be able to make things a bit difficult for me. But I
said to myself, "Come, Gascon, do what has to be done.
Onward, Cyrano!" A moment later, someone . . .

CHRISTIAN

Nosed you out in the darkness.

CYRANO

. . . lunged at me with his sword. I parried the thrust
and suddenly found myself . . .

CHRISTIAN

Nose to nose . . .

CYRANO

(Rushing toward him)

No! By all the saints in heaven, I'll . . . *(The Gascons
crowd forward to see better, but as soon as he is in front
of* CHRISTIAN *he again controls himself and continues his
story.)* I found myself facing a hundred shouting brutes,
all smelling . . .

CHRISTIAN

With their noses, of course.

CYRANO

(Smiling wanly)

. . . of onions and cheap wine. I plunged into the midst
of them . . .

CHRISTIAN

Nose first!

CYRANO

. . . and immediately cut down two of them. As I was attacking a third, I saw a sword . . .

CHRISTIAN

Right under your nose!

CYRANO
(Bellowing)
Out! All of you! Get out!
(The CADETS *all hurry toward the doors.)*

FIRST CADET

The tiger has finally awakened!

CYRANO

Leave me alone with this man!

SECOND CADET

He'll soon be turned into mincemeat!

RAGUENEAU

Mincemeat?

THIRD CADET

Yes, ready to be baked in one of your pie crusts!

RAGUENEAU

I feel faint, and limp as a napkin!

CARBON

Let's go.

FOURTH CADET

There won't be anything left of him!

FIFTH CADET

It makes me tremble just to think of what's going to happen to him!

SIXTH CADET
(Closing the door on the right as he goes out)
It will be something horrifying!
(They have all left, most of them through the doors at the sides and in the background, with a few having disappeared up the stairs. CHRISTIAN *and* CYRANO *are left standing face to face. They look at each other for a moment.)*

Scene X

Cyrano, Christian.

CYRANO

Embrace me!

CHRISTIAN

Sir . . .

CYRANO

You're a brave man.

CHRISTIAN

Perhaps, but . . .

CYRANO

Very brave. I'm glad to know that.

CHRISTIAN

Would you mind telling me . . .

CYRANO

Embrace me. I'm her brother.

CHRISTIAN

Whose brother?

CYRANO

Hers!

CHRISTIAN

Hers?

CYRANO

Roxane's!

CHRISTIAN
(Hurrying toward him)
Oh! You? Her brother?

CYRANO

Yes, or almost. A brotherly cousin.

CHRISTIAN

And she's told you . . .

CYRANO

Everything!

CHRISTIAN

Does she love me?

CYRANO

Perhaps!

CHRISTIAN
(Taking his hands)
How happy I am to know you!

CYRANO

That's a rather sudden change of feeling.

CHRISTIAN

Forgive me. . . .

CYRANO
(Looks at him and puts his hands on his shoulders.)
It's true: you *are* a handsome devil!

CHRISTIAN

If you only knew, sir, how much I admire you!

CYRANO

But all those "noses" you gave me . . .

CHRISTIAN

I take them all back!

CYRANO

Roxane expects to receive a letter from you this evening.

CHRISTIAN

Oh, no!

CYRANO

What? . . .

CHRISTIAN

If I write to her, she'll never want to see me again.

CYRANO

Why?

CHRISTIAN

Because I'm such a fool that I could die of shame!

CYRANO

No, you're not, since you've said it yourself. Besides, you didn't attack me like a fool.

CHRISTIAN

Words come easily to anyone when he wants to pick a quarrel. I may have a certain quick, soldierly wit, but with women I'm always at a loss for anything to say. Their eyes show interest when I pass by, but . . .

CYRANO

Aren't their hearts also interested when you stop?

CHRISTIAN

No! It's all too clear to me that I'm one of those men who don't know how to speak of love.

CYRANO

I have the feeling that if my features had been shaped more harmoniously, I would have been one of those men who *do* know how to speak of love.

CHRISTIAN

Ah, if only I could express myself gracefully!

CYRANO

If only I had a handsome face!

CHRISTIAN

Roxane is so elegant and refined—I'm sure to disillusion her!

CYRANO

(Looking at CHRISTIAN*)*
If I had such an interpreter to speak for my soul . . .

CHRISTIAN

(Despairingly)
I need eloquence, and I have none!

CYRANO

(Abruptly)
I'll lend you mine! Lend me your conquering physical charm, and together we'll form a romantic hero!

CHRISTIAN

What do you mean?

CYRANO

Do you feel capable of repeating what I tell you every day?

CHRISTIAN

Are you suggesting . . .

CYRANO

Roxane won't be disillusioned! Together, we can win her heart! Will you let my soul pass from my leather jerkin and lodge beneath your embroidered doublet?

CHRISTIAN

But Cyrano . . .

CYRANO

Are you willing?

CHRISTIAN

You frighten me!

CYRANO

Your only fear is that you'll chill her heart when you speak to her, but if she hears my words from your lips, she'll soon be aflame!

CHRISTIAN

Your eyes are shining. . . .

CYRANO

Will you do it?

CHRISTIAN

Would it please you so much?

CYRANO

(Ardently)
It would . . . *(Restrains himself and adopts a more detached tone.)* It would amuse me! It's an experiment that would tempt any poet. Shall we complete each other? We'll walk together: you in the light, I in the shadows. I'll make you eloquent, you'll make me handsome.

CHRISTIAN

But I must write her a letter without delay! I'll never be able to . . .

CYRANO
(Taking out the letter he has written)
Here's your letter!

CHRISTIAN
What . . .

CYRANO
It lacks only the name and address.

CHRISTIAN
I . . .

CYRANO
You can send it as it is. Don't worry, it's well written.

CHRISTIAN
Had you already . . .

CYRANO
I always have a letter in my pocket, written to some imaginary lady, because I'm one of those men whose only sweethearts are dreams breathed into the bubble of a name. You can change my fantasy to reality. You can take my vows and pleas, launched at random into the empty air, and give them all a single destination. You'll see that in this letter my feelings are all the better expressed for being insincere! Here, take it.

CHRISTIAN
Won't some things in it have to be changed? Since you wrote it with no specific woman in mind, how can it fit Roxane?

CYRANO
It will fit her like a glove!

CHRISTIAN
But . . .

CYRANO
You can count on vanity to make her think it was written for her!

CHRISTIAN
Ah, my friend! . . .

(He throws himself into CYRANO'S *arms. They stand embracing each other.)*

Scene XI

Cyrano, Christian, the Gascons, the Musketeer, Lise.

A CADET
(Pushing the door ajar)
Nothing. . . . A deathly silence. . . . I'm afraid to look. . . .
(Puts his head through the doorway.) What!

ALL THE CADETS
(Entering and seeing CYRANO *and* CHRISTIAN *embracing each other)*
Oh!—Ah!

A CADET
I can't believe my eyes!
(Consternation)

THE MUSKETEER
(Jeeringly)
Well, look at that!

CARBON
Our demon has become as gentle as a lamb! When he's struck on one nostril, he turns the other!

THE MUSKETEER
He lets people talk about his nose now? *(Calls out to* LISE, *with a triumphant expression.)* Lise! Watch this! *(Approaches* CYRANO *and insolently stares at his nose.)* What's that long thing on your face, sir? It reminds me of something, but I can't recall what it is.

CYRANO
Then let me help you by jarring your memory!
(Slaps him. The CADETS *are delighted to see* CYRANO *behaving like himself again. They caper joyfully.)*

CURTAIN

Act Three

Roxane's Kiss

A little square in the Marais quarter of Paris. Old houses and a perspective of narrow streets. To the right, ROXANE's house and the wall of its garden, overflowing with foliage. Above the door, a window and a balcony. A bench in front of the threshold.

Ivy on the wall. The balcony is garlanded with quivering, drooping jasmine.

By means of the bench and the jutting stones of the wall, one can easily climb up to the balcony.

Opposite, another old house in the same style, made of brick and stone, with an entrance door. The knocker of this door is wrapped in cloth like an injured thumb.

As the curtain rises, the DUENNA is seated on the bench. The window is open wide onto ROXANE's balcony.

Beside the DUENNA stands RAGUENEAU, dressed in a kind of livery. He is finishing a story, and wiping his eyes.

Scene I

Ragueneau, the Duenna, then Roxane, Cyrano, and two Pages.

RAGUENEAU

. . . and then she ran off with a musketeer! Alone and ruined, I felt I had nothing to live for, so I tried to hang myself, but Monsieur de Bergerac came in and cut me down. Then he offered me this position as his cousin's steward.

THE DUENNA

But how did you come to be ruined?

RAGUENEAU

Lise liked warriors and I liked poets. Mars ate everything that Apollo left. At that rate, it didn't take long!

THE DUENNA

(Standing up and calling toward the open window)
Roxane, are you ready? We're late!

ROXANE'S VOICE

(From the window)
I'm just putting on my cloak!

THE DUENNA

(To RAGUENEAU, *pointing to the door opposite)*
That's where we're going, to Clomire's. She holds regular discussion meetings in her house. A discourse on the Tender Passion will be read today.

RAGUENEAU

The Tender Passion?

THE DUENNA

(Simpering)
Yes, that's right. *(Shouts toward the window.)* Roxane! Hurry or we'll miss the discourse on the Tender Passion!

ROXANE'S VOICE

I'm coming!
(A sound of stringed instruments is heard approaching.)

CYRANO'S VOICE

(Singing offstage)
La-la-la-la . . .

THE DUENNA
(Surprised)
Is someone coming to play for us?

CYRANO
(Entering, followed by two PAGES carrying lutes)
Those are thirty-second notes, you fool!

FIRST PAGE
(Ironically)
Ah, so you know about thirty-second notes, sir!

CYRANO
I'm a musician, like all of Gassendi's* disciples!

THE PAGE
(Playing and singing)
La-la . . .

CYRANO
(Takes the lute away from him and continues the melody.)
Let me do it! La-la-la-la . . .

ROXANE
(Appearing on the balcony)
Ah, it's you!

CYRANO
(Singing his words to the melody)
I've come to salute your lilies, and pay my respects to your roses!

ROXANE
I'm coming down!
(Leaves the balcony.)

THE DUENNA
(Pointing to the PAGES)
Where did these two virtuosi come from?

CYRANO
I won them from d'Assoucy on a bet. We were arguing

---

* Pierre Gassendi (1592–1655), French mathematician and philosopher. The real Cyrano is said to have studied with him, but there is no certain evidence of it.

about a point of grammar when suddenly he pointed to these lute-playing louts, who always accompany him wherever he goes, and said to me, "I'll bet you a day of music!" He lost, and therefore ordered them to follow me and bear harmonious witness to everything I do until tomorrow. It was charming at first, but it has already begun to pall. *(To the* PAGES*)* Go and serenade Montfleury, and tell him I sent you! *(The* PAGES *go upstage to leave.* CYRANO *turns back to the* DUENNA.*)* I've come to ask Roxane, as I do every day . . . *(To the* PAGES*, as they are leaving)* Play a long time—and off-key! *(To the* DUENNA*)* . . . whether her soulmate is still a model of perfection.

ROXANE
(Coming out of the house)
Oh, he's so handsome! And such a brilliant mind! I can't tell you how much I love him!

CYRANO
(Smiling)
You feel that Christian has a brilliant mind?

ROXANE
Even more brilliant than yours!

CYRANO
I won't contest that.

ROXANE
I don't believe there's anyone in the world who can match him in saying those sweet nothings that mean everything. Sometimes he seems distracted and his inspiration falters, then all at once he says exquisite things to me!

CYRANO
(Incredulously)
Really?

ROXANE
Just like a man! Because he's handsome, you think he has to be dull-witted!

CYRANO
Does he speak well about matters of the heart?

ROXANE

Not well—superbly!

CYRANO

And how does he write?

ROXANE

Even better than he speaks! Just listen to this! *(Declaiming)* "The more you take of my heart, the more I have!" *(Triumphantly)* There, what do you think of that?

CYRANO

(Unenthusiastically)
Oh . . .

ROXANE

And this: "Since I need a heart with which to suffer, if you keep mine, send me yours!"

CYRANO

First he has too much heart, then not enough. He can't seem to make up his mind.

ROXANE

(Stamping her foot)
You're exasperating! You only talk like that because you're jealous . . .

CYRANO

(Starting)
What?

ROXANE

. . . of the way he writes! Listen to this and tell me if you think anything could be more tender: "Believe me when I say that my heart cries out to you, and that if kisses could be sent in writing, you would read this letter with your lips."

CYRANO

(Smiling with satisfaction in spite of himself)
Well, those lines are . . . *(Catches himself and continues in a disdainful tone.)* . . . rather affected.

ROXANE

And listen to this. . . .

CYRANO
(Delighted)
You know all his letters by heart?

ROXANE
Every one of them!

CYRANO
(Twisting his mustache)
That's quite flattering.

ROXANE
He's a master of eloquence!

CYRANO
(Modestly)
Let's not exaggerate. . . .

ROXANE
(Peremptorily)
A master!

CYRANO
(Bowing)
Very well, then, a master!

THE DUENNA
(Hurrying downstage, after having gone upstage earlier)
Monsieur de Guiche is coming! *(To* CYRANO, *pushing him toward the house)* Go inside! It will be better for him not to find you here; it might put him on the scent. . . .

ROXANE
(To CYRANO*)*
Yes, on the scent of my precious secret! He's in love with me and he's powerful—he mustn't know! He might strike a cruel blow at my love for Christian!

CYRANO
(Entering the house)
I'll do as you wish.
*(*DE GUICHE *appears.)*

Scene II

Roxane, De Guiche, the Duenna in the background.

ROXANE
(To DE GUICHE, *with a curtsey)*
We were about to leave. . . .

DE GUICHE
I've come to say good-by.

ROXANE
You're going away?

DE GUICHE
Yes. To war.

ROXANE
Ah!

DE GUICHE
I'm leaving tonight.

ROXANE
Ah!

DE GUICHE
I have my orders. We're besieging Arras.*

ROXANE
Ah! A siege?

DE GUICHE
Yes. . . . My departure seems to leave you cold.

ROXANE
(Politely)
Not at all.

DE GUICHE
For my part, I'm heartbroken. Will I ever see you again?
If so, when? . . . Do you know that I've been made
a colonel?

---

* A city, now in France, which was captured by the French from
the Spanish in 1640, when it was part of the Spanish Netherlands.

ROXANE

(With indifference)
Congratulations.

DE GUICHE

And I'm in command of the Guards.

ROXANE

(Startled)
The Guards?

DE GUICHE

Yes, the regiment in which your boastful cousin serves.
I'll find a way to take revenge on him when we're at
Arras.

ROXANE

(Choking)
What! The Guards are being sent there?

DE GUICHE

(Laughing)
Of course: that's my regiment!
    (ROXANE sits down heavily on the bench.)

ROXANE

(Aside)
Christian! . . .

DE GUICHE

What's the matter?

ROXANE

(Overwhelmed with emotion)
I'm in despair at . . . at what you've told me. . . . When
a woman cares for a man and learns that he's going
to war . . .

DE GUICHE

(Surprised and delighted)
Why did you wait for the day of my departure to say
such a tender thing to me for the first time?

ROXANE

(Changing her tone and fanning herself)
So you're going to take revenge on my cousin?

DE GUICHE

(Smiling)
Do you side with him?

ROXANE

No—against him!

DE GUICHE

Do you see him?

ROXANE

Very seldom.

DE GUICHE

He's seen everywhere with one of the Cadets . . . *(Tries to think of the name.)* . . . a young man named Neu . . . Neuvillen . . . Neuviller . . .

ROXANE

Tall?

DE GUICHE

Yes, with blond hair.

ROXANE

Reddish blond.

DE GUICHE

And handsome.

ROXANE

Not very.

DE GUICHE

But stupid.

ROXANE

He looks like it. *(Changing her tone)* Are you planning to take revenge on Cyrano by exposing him to the fire of the enemy? If so, you'll get little satisfaction from it, because he loves danger! I know how you could really make him suffer!

DE GUICHE

How?

ROXANE

Leave him behind with his dear Cadets when the regi-

ment goes off to fight. Make him sit idly in Paris through
the whole war! That's the best way to torment a man
like him. If you want to punish him, deprive him of
danger!

DE GUICHE

Only a woman could have thought of a trick like that!

ROXANE

He'll eat his heart out at not being in action, his friends
will angrily chew their fingernails, and you'll be avenged.

DE GUICHE

(Drawing closer)

Then you do love me a little! *(She smiles.)* I like to think
that your sharing my rancor is a sign of love, Roxane!

ROXANE

It is.

DE GUICHE

(Showing her several sealed envelopes)

I have orders that will be delivered to each company
without delay, except . . . *(Separates one of them from
the others.)* . . . for this one, addressed to the Cadets!
(Puts it in his pocket.) I'll keep it. *(Laughing)* Ha, ha,
Cyrano! We'll see how your warlike temperament takes
to this! . . . Tell me, Roxane, do you sometimes play
tricks on people yourself?

ROXANE

(Looking at him)

Yes, sometimes.

DE GUICHE

(Close to her)

You drive me mad! I intended to leave tonight, but how
can I part from you when you've just revealed such feelings to me? Listen. . . . Near here, on the Rue d'Orléans,
there's a monastery founded by the syndic of the Capuchins, Father Athanare. Laymen aren't allowed to enter
it, but I'll see to it that the good monks make an excep-
tion in my case. Their sleeves are wide enough to let me
hide in them! The Capuchins serve Cardinal Richelieu
directly; their awe of the uncle makes them fear the

nephew. Everyone will believe I've left Paris. I'll then come to you, masked. Let me delay my departure one day!

ROXANE

(Anxiously)

But if it becomes known, your glory will be . . .

DE GUICHE

Have no fear!

ROXANE

But the siege of Arras . . .

DE GUICHE

Never mind! Let me do it!

ROXANE

No!

DE GUICHE

Let me!

ROXANE

(Tenderly)

I must refuse.

DE GUICHE

Ah!

ROXANE

Go! *(Aside)* And Christian will stay. *(To* DE GUICHE*)* I want you to be heroic . . . Antoine!

DE GUICHE

What heavenly words! Do you love . . .

ROXANE

Yes, I love the man for whom I fear.

DE GUICHE

(Overjoyed)

I'm going now! *(Kisses her hand.)* Are you satisfied?

ROXANE

Yes, Antoine.

(He leaves.)

THE DUENNA
(Bowing comically to him behind his back)
Yes, Antoine!

ROXANE
(To the DUENNA)
Don't say a word about what I've done. Cyrano would
never forgive me if he knew I'd robbed him of his war!
(Calls toward the house.) Cousin!

Scene III

Roxane, the Duenna, Cyrano.

ROXANE
We're going to Clomire's house. *(Points to the door opposite.)* Alcandre and Lysimon are going to speak there!

THE DUENNA
Yes, but something tells me that we're going to miss
them.

CYRANO
(To ROXANE)
I wouldn't want you to miss those parrots.
(They have arrived in front of CLOMIRE's door.)

THE DUENNA
(With delight)
Oh, look! The knocker is wrapped in cloth! *(To the
knocker)* You've been gagged, you metallic little brute,
to prevent you from disturbing the noble speeches!
(Carefully lifts it and knocks gently.)

ROXANE
(Seeing that the door is being opened)
Let's go inside! *(From the threshold, to CYRANO)* If
Christian comes, as I presume he will, tell him to wait
for me.

CYRANO
(Quickly, as she is about to disappear)
One moment! *(She turns back toward him.)* You always

have a subject on which you question him; what will it be this time?

ROXANE

This time . . .

CYRANO

(Eagerly)
Yes?

ROXANE

You won't tell him?

CYRANO

I'll be as silent as a tomb.

ROXANE

Well, this time I'm not going to question him about anything! I'll say to him, "Give free rein to your mind! Improvise! Speak to me of love in your magnificent way!"

CYRANO

(Smiling)
Good.

ROXANE

Sh!

CYRANO

Sh!

ROXANE

Not a word!
    (Goes inside and closes the door behind her.)

CYRANO

(Bowing to her, after the door is closed)
I thank you.
    (The door opens again and ROXANE's *head appears.)*

ROXANE

If he knew, he might prepare a speech in advance!

CYRANO

Do you really think so?

BOTH TOGETHER

Sh!

(The door closes.)

CYRANO

(Calling)
Christian!

Scene IV

Cyrano, Christian.

CYRANO

I know what we need to know. Prepare your memory:
here's a chance to cover yourself with glory! Why are
you looking so unhappy? Come, there's no time to lose!
We'll hurry to your house and I'll tell you . . .

CHRISTIAN

No!

CYRANO

What?

CHRISTIAN

No! I'm going to wait for Roxane here.

CYRANO

Have you lost your reason? Come with me, you must
learn . . .

CHRISTIAN

No, I tell you! I'm tired of borrowing my letters and
speeches, of always playing a part and trembling lest I
forget my lines! It was necessary at the beginning and
I'm grateful to you for your help, but now that I feel
she really loves me, I'm no longer afraid. I'm going to
speak for myself.

CYRANO

(Ironically)
Do you believe that's a good idea?

CHRISTIAN

What makes you think I can't do it? After all, I'm not so stupid! You'll see! Your lessons haven't been wasted on me, my friend: I'm sure I can speak without your guidance now. And in any case I'll certainly know how to take her in my arms! *(Sees* ROXANE *coming out of* CLOMIRE's *house.)* Here she comes! No, Cyrano, don't leave me!

CYRANO

(Bowing to him)
Speak for yourself, sir.
(Disappears behind the garden wall.)

Scene V

Christian, Roxane, and briefly, the Duenna and several intellectual ladies and gentlemen.

ROXANE

(Coming out of CLOMIRE's *house with the other guests and exchanging farewell bows with them)*
Good-by, Barthénoïde . . . Alcandre . . . Grémione . . .

THE DUENNA

(Despairingly)
We missed the discourse on the Tender Passion!
(Goes into ROXANE's *house.)*

ROXANE

(Still bowing)
Urimédonte . . . Good-by! *(They all bow to her and to each other, then separate and go off in different directions. She sees* CHRISTIAN.*)* Ah, it's you! *(Goes to him.)* Dusk is gathering. Wait. . . . They're far away now. The air is pleasant and no one is passing by. Let's sit down. Talk to me. I'm listening.
*(*CHRISTIAN *sits down beside her on the bench. There is a silence.)*

CHRISTIAN

I love you.

ROXANE

(Closing her eyes)
Yes, speak to me of love.

CHRISTIAN

I love you.

ROXANE

That's the theme—now elaborate on it.

CHRISTIAN

I love . . .

ROXANE

Develop your theme!

CHRISTIAN

I love you so much!

ROXANE

Go on.

CHRISTIAN

I . . . I'd be so happy if you loved me! Tell me that you
do, Roxane!

ROXANE

(Pouting)
You're giving me water when I expected cream! Tell me
how you love me.

CHRISTIAN

I love you . . . very much!

ROXANE

Surely you can express your feelings better than that!

CHRISTIAN

*(Who has moved closer to her and is now devouring
her neck with his eyes)*
Your neck! I'd like to kiss it. . . .

ROXANE

Christian!

CHRISTIAN

I love you!

ROXANE
(Starting to stand up)
Again!

CHRISTIAN
(Quickly, holding her back)
No, I don't love you!

ROXANE
(Sitting down again)
At least that's a change.

CHRISTIAN
I adore you!

ROXANE
(Standing up and moving away)
Oh!

CHRISTIAN
Yes. . . . I'm becoming foolish!

ROXANE
(Curtly)
And it displeases me! As it would displease me if you
became ugly.

CHRISTIAN
But . . .

ROXANE
Try to bring back your vanished eloquence!

CHRISTIAN
I . . .

ROXANE
I know: you love me. Good-by.
(Goes toward the house.)

CHRISTIAN
Wait! Let me tell you . . .

ROXANE
(Opening the door)
That you adore me? I already know that. No, no! Go
away!

CHRISTIAN

But I . . .
(She closes the door in his face.)

CYRANO
*(Who has returned a short time earlier without being
seen)*
Congratulations on your success.

Scene VI

Christian, Cyrano, the Pages briefly.

CHRISTIAN

Help me!

CYRANO

No.

CHRISTIAN

If I don't win her back immediately, I'll die!

CYRANO

How the devil do you expect me to teach you
immediately . . .

CHRISTIAN
(Gripping his arm)
Oh! Look!
(A light has appeared in the balcony window.)

CYRANO
(With deep emotion)
Her window!

CHRISTIAN
(Shouting)
I'll die!

CYRANO

Lower your voice!

CHRISTIAN
(Softly)
I'll die. . . .

CYRANO

It's dark now.

CHRISTIAN

What of it?

CYRANO

The damage can be repaired. You don't deserve . . .
Stand here, in front of the balcony, you wretched fool!
I'll be under it, telling you what to say.

CHRISTIAN

But . . .

CYRANO

Quiet!
(The PAGES appear in the background.)

THE PAGES

(To CYRANO)
Here we are!

CYRANO

Sh!
(Signals them to speak softly.)

FIRST PAGE

(In an undertone)
We've been serenading Montfleury!

CYRANO

(Quickly, also in an undertone)
I want you to stand watch, one at that corner, the other
at that one. If you see anyone coming, begin playing
your lutes.

SECOND PAGE

What shall we play, noble disciple of Gassendi?

CYRANO

A happy melody for a woman, a sad one for a man. *(The
PAGES disappear, one toward each street corner. CYRANO
speaks to CHRISTIAN.)* Call her!

CHRISTIAN

Roxane!

CYRANO
(Picking up pebbles and throwing them against the window)
Just a moment. First, a few pebbles. . . .

Scene VII

Roxane, Christian, Cyrano, hidden at first under the balcony.

ROXANE
(Partially opening her window)
Who's there?

CHRISTIAN
It's I.

ROXANE
Who?

CHRISTIAN
Christian.

ROXANE
(With disdain)
Oh, it's you.

CHRISTIAN
I'd like to speak to you.

CYRANO
(Under the balcony, to CHRISTIAN*)*
That's good. Keep your voice down.

ROXANE
No! You speak too awkwardly. Go away.

CHRISTIAN
Please. . . .

ROXANE
No! You've stopped loving me!

CHRISTIAN
(Repeating what CYRANO *tells him)*
Impossible! . . . I could no more . . . stop loving you . . .
than I could stop . . . the rising of the sun!

ROXANE
(Pausing just as she was about to close the window)
Ah! That's better!

CHRISTIAN
(Still repeating CYRANO*'s words)*
My cruel love . . . has never ceased to grow . . . in
my tormented soul . . . since the day . . . when it was
born there.

ROXANE
(Coming out onto the balcony)
That's better! . . . But since your love is cruel, you were
foolish not to smother it at birth.

CHRISTIAN
(Still repeating)
I tried, without success. . . . It had the strength of
Hercules . . . from the first moment of its life.

ROXANE
That's better!

CHRISTIAN
(Still repeating)
And so it strangled . . . without effort . . . the two
serpents . . . of Pride and Doubt.

ROXANE
*(Leaning forward with her elbows on the railing of
the balcony)*
Very good! . . . But why do you speak so haltingly? Has
your imagination gone lame?

CYRANO
(Pulling CHRISTIAN *under the balcony and taking
his place)*
Sh! This is becoming too difficult!

ROXANE
Your words are hesitant tonight. Why?

CYRANO
(Speaking softly, like CHRISTIAN)
Because of the darkness, they must grope their way to
your ears.

ROXANE
My words have no such difficulty.

CYRANO
They go straight to my heart, a goal too large to miss,
whereas your ears are small. And your words travel
swiftly because they fall, while mine must slowly climb.

ROXANE
But they seem to be climbing better now.

CYRANO
They've finally become accustomed to that exercise.

ROXANE
It's true that I'm speaking from high above you.

CYRANO
Yes, and it would kill me if you let a harsh word fall on
my heart from that height!

ROXANE
(Making a movement)
I'll come down to you!

CYRANO
(Urgently)
No!

ROXANE
(Pointing to the bench below the balcony)
Then climb up on that bench.

CYRANO
(Stepping back into the shadows in alarm)
No!

ROXANE
Why not?

CYRANO
(Increasingly overcome by emotion)
I want to go on taking advantage of this opportunity . . .

this chance for us to talk quietly . . . without seeing each other.

ROXANE

Why should we talk without seeing each other?

CYRANO

I find it delightful. We're almost invisible to each other. You see the blackness of a long cloak, I see the whiteness of a summer dress. I'm only a shadow, you're only a spot of brightness. You can't know what these moments mean to me! I may sometimes have been eloquent in the past . . .

ROXANE

You have!

CYRANO

. . . but until now my words have never come from my true heart.

ROXANE

Why?

CYRANO

Because . . . till now I always spoke through . . .

ROXANE

Through what?

CYRANO

The intoxication that seizes anyone who stands before your gaze! . . . But tonight it seems to me that I'm speaking to you for the first time.

ROXANE

Perhaps it's true—even your voice is different.

CYRANO
(Impetuously moving closer)
Yes, quite different, because in the protecting darkness I dare at last to be myself, I dare . . . *(Pauses, then continues distractedly.)* What was I saying? I don't know. . . . All this . . . Excuse my agitation! All this is so enchanting . . . so new to me!

ROXANE

So new?

CYRANO

(Deeply stirred, and still trying to cover up what he has admitted)

Yes, it's new to me to be sincere . . . without fear of being laughed at. . . .

ROXANE

Laughed at for what?

CYRANO

For . . . for an outburst of feeling! My heart always timidly hides itself behind my mind. I set out to bring down stars from the sky, then, for fear of ridicule, I stop and pick little flowers of eloquence.

ROXANE

Those little flowers have their charm.

CYRANO

Yes, but let's scorn them tonight!

ROXANE

You've never talked to me like this before.

CYRANO

I'd like to turn away from Cupid and his arrows, and go with you toward . . . fresher things! Rather than daintily sipping stale sentimentality from ornate golden cups, let's try to learn how the soul slakes its thirst by drinking directly from the great river of love!

ROXANE

But you yourself . . .

CYRANO

Yes, I used pretty phrases at first, to make you listen to me, but now it would be an insult to this fragrant night, this moment, and nature herself, if I were to speak with the affected elegance of a courtly love letter! One look at the starry sky above us is enough to make me want to throw off all artificiality. If the expression of feeling is refined too much, the feeling itself is lost. The soul is emptied by such vain pastimes, and love dies, smothered under a mass of flowery words that were meant to embellish it.

ROXANE

But it seems to me that elegant language . . .

CYRANO

It has no place in true love! It's only a game, and those
who love will suffer if they play it too long. For most of
them there comes a time—and I pity those for whom it
doesn't come!—when they feel a noble love inside themselves that's saddened by every grandiloquent word they say.

ROXANE

Well, if that time has come for us, what words will you
say to me?

CYRANO

All those that enter my mind of their own accord. I'll
give them to you as they come, without arranging them
in bouquets: I love you, I'm overwhelmed, I love you to
the point of madness! Your name is in my heart like a
bell shaken by my constant trembling, ringing day and
night: Roxane, Roxane, Roxane! Loving everything
about you, I forget nothing. I remember the day last
year, the twelfth of May, when you wore your hair in a
different style. Just as a man who has looked at the sun
too long sees red circles everywhere, when I've gazed
on the bright glory of your hair my dazzled eyes see
golden spots on everything!

ROXANE

(In a tremulous voice)
Yes, that's really love. . . .

CYRANO

Of course! The feeling that holds me in its merciless grip
could be nothing else but love! It has all the terrible
jealousy and somber violence of love, and all the un-
selfishness, too. How gladly I would give my happiness
for the sake of yours, even without your knowledge, ask-
ing only to hear from a distance, now and then, the
laughter born of my sacrifice! Each time I look at you,
you strengthen my courage and bring forth some new
virtue. Are you beginning to understand now? Do you
feel my soul rising to you in the darkness? Ah, it's all
too beautiful, too sweet, this evening! I say all these

things and you listen to me—*you* listen to *me*! It's more than my poor heart can bear! Even in my most daring dreams I never hoped for so much! I could die happily at this moment! It's because of my words that you're trembling—for you *are* trembling, like one of the leaves in the dark foliage above me: I've felt the beloved tremor of your hand descending along the jasmine branches!

(Fervently kisses the end of a drooping branch.)

ROXANE

Yes, I'm trembling, and I'm weeping, and I love you, and I'm yours! You've made me drunk with love!

CYRANO

Then let death come, now that I've aroused such feelings in you! I ask only one thing . . .

CHRISTIAN
(From under the balcony)
A kiss!

ROXANE
(Quickly drawing back)
What?

CYRANO

Oh!

ROXANE

You ask . . .

CYRANO

Yes, I . . . *(To* CHRISTIAN, *in an undertone)* You're going too fast!

CHRISTIAN

She's in a willing mood—I must take advantage of it!

CYRANO
(To ROXANE*)*
Yes, I . . . I asked for a kiss, but I now realize that I was much too bold.

ROXANE
(A little disappointed)
You don't insist?

CYRANO

Yes, I insist . . . but not insistently! I've offended your modesty. . . . Don't give me that kiss!

CHRISTIAN

(To CYRANO, tugging at his cloak)
Why do you say that?

CYRANO

Quiet, Christian!

ROXANE

(Leaning forward)
What are you saying?

CYRANO

I was scolding myself for having gone too far. I just said to myself, "Quiet, Christian!" *(The lutes begin playing.)* Wait! Someone's coming! *(ROXANE closes the window. CYRANO listens to the lutes: one of them is playing gaily, the other mournfully.)* A sad tune and a happy one, both at the same time? What do they mean? Is it a man or a woman? . . . Ah! It's a Capuchin!
(A CAPUCHIN enters; holding a lantern in his hand, he goes from house to house, looking at the doors.)

Scene VIII

Cyrano, Christian, a Capuchin.

CYRANO

(To the CAPUCHIN)
What are you doing? Renewing Diogenes's search?

THE CAPUCHIN

I'm looking for the house of Madame . . .

CHRISTIAN

What a nuisance!

THE CAPUCHIN

Magdeleine Robin.

CHRISTIAN

What does he want?

CYRANO

(To the CAPUCHIN, *showing him an uphill street)*
It's that way. Straight ahead.

THE CAPUCHIN

Thank you. I'll say all the prayers in my rosary for you.
(He leaves.)

CYRANO

Good luck! May my best wishes go with you!
(Returns to CHRISTIAN.*)*

Scene IX

Cyrano, Christian.

CHRISTIAN

You must get that kiss for me!

CYRANO

No!

CHRISTIAN

Sooner or later . . .

CYRANO

Yes, it's true. Sooner or later there will be an ecstatic
moment when your mouths are drawn together, because
of your blond mustache and her pink lips! *(To himself)*
I prefer it to be because of . . .
(Sound of the window being opened again. CHRIS-
TIAN *hides under the balcony.)*

Scene X

Cyrano, Christian, Roxane.

ROXANE

(Coming out onto the balcony)
Are you still there? We were talking about . . . about a . . .

CYRANO

A kiss. The word is so sweet! Why should you be afraid to say it? If even the word burns your lips, what will the act do? Don't be alarmed; you've already given up your bantering tone and gradually drifted from smiles to sighs, and then from sighs to tears! Let yourself drift a little further: you'll cross the distance from tears to a kiss in the time it takes for one quiver of joy!

ROXANE

Stop!

CYRANO

After all, what is a kiss? A vow made at closer range, a more precise promise, a confession that contains its own proof, a seal placed on a pact that has already been signed; it's a secret told to the mouth rather than to the ear, a fleeting moment filled with the hush of eternity, a communion that has the fragrance of a flower, a way of living by the beat of another heart, and tasting another soul on one's lips!

ROXANE

Stop!

CYRANO

Kisses are so noble that the Queen of France once gave one to an English lord!

ROXANE

But I don't see . . .

CYRANO
(Becoming more impassioned)
Like the Duke of Buckingham, I've suffered in silence; like him, I worship a queen;* like him, I'm sad and faithful. . . .

ROXANE

And like him, you're handsome!

* George Villiers, Duke of Buckingham (1592–1629), was in love with the Queen of France, Anne of Austria (1601–66), wife of Louis XIII. Alexandre Dumas wrote a fictionalized version of their romance in *The Three Musketeers.*

CYRANO
(Aside, abruptly sobered)
Ah, yes, I'm handsome; I was forgetting that. . . .

ROXANE
Come to me! Come and give me that matchless flower . . .

CYRANO
(Pushing CHRISTIAN *toward the balcony)*
Climb up to her!

ROXANE
. . . that communion . . .

CYRANO
Climb!

ROXANE
. . . that hush of eternity . . .

CYRANO
Climb!

CHRISTIAN
(Hesitating)
But now it seems to me that it's wrong!

ROXANE
. . . that taste of another soul!

CYRANO
(Pushing him)
Climb, you fool!
*(*CHRISTIAN *stands on the bench, then climbs up onto the balcony.)*

CHRISTIAN
Ah, Roxane!
(Takes her in his arms and kisses her.)

CYRANO
What a strange pang in my heart! I'm like Lazarus at the feast—a feast of love! I must content myself with very little, but I still have a few small crumbs. Yes, I feel something of that kiss in my heart, because Roxane is kissing not only Christian's lips, but also the words I spoke to her! *(The lutes begin playing again.)* A sad tune and a happy one: the Capuchin! *(Takes a few rapid steps, pretending to have just arrived, and calls out loudly.)* Roxane!

ROXANE

Who is it?

CYRANO

It's I. I was passing by. . . . Is Christian still here?

CHRISTIAN

(Surprised)
Cyrano!

ROXANE

Good evening, cousin.

CYRANO

Good evening, cousin.

ROXANE

I'm coming down!
(She disappears into the house. The CAPUCHIN *enters in the background.)*

CHRISTIAN

(Seeing him)
No! Not again!
(Follows ROXANE.)

Scene XI

Cyrano, Christian, Roxane, the Capuchin, Ragueneau.

THE CAPUCHIN

This is Magdeleine Robin's house!

CYRANO

You said "Rolin" before.

THE CAPUCHIN

No, I said "Robin!" R-O-B-I-N!

ROXANE

(Appearing in the doorway of the house, followed by RAGUENEAU, *who carries a lantern, and* CHRISTIAN)
Who's this?

THE CAPUCHIN

I have a letter for you.

CHRISTIAN

A letter?

THE CAPUCHIN

(To ROXANE*)*
It surely concerns some holy matter. It's from a worthy
lord who . . .

ROXANE

(To CHRISTIAN*)*
It's from De Guiche!

CHRISTIAN

How dare he . . .

ROXANE

He won't bother me much longer! *(Opening the letter)* I
love you, and if . . . *(By the light of* RAGUENEAU*'s lantern, she reads the letter to herself in a low voice.)* "The
drums are beating and my regiment is preparing to
leave. Everyone believes that I have already gone, but I
am staying, in disobedience to your orders. I am in a
monastery. This letter is to inform you that I will soon
come to visit you. The monk who will deliver it to you
is as simpleminded as a goat, so there is no danger of
his guessing my plan. Your lips have smiled at me too
much today; I must see them again. I hope that you have
already forgiven my boldness, and I remain your . . ."
And so on. *(To the* CAPUCHIN*)* Father, you must hear
what's in this letter. Listen. *(The others gather around
her and she pretends to read aloud.)* "You must bow to
the Cardinal's will, however difficult it may be for you.
This letter will be delivered into your charming hands
by a saintly, intelligent, and discreet Capuchin. You will
inform him that we wish him to give you the blessing of
holy matrimony . . ." *(Turns the page.)* ". . . in your
house, and without delay. Christian must secretly become your husband. I have already sent him to you. I
know that you dislike him, but you must accept the
Cardinal's decision, and you may rest assured that
heaven will bless you for your resignation. With the re-
spect that I have always borne for you, I remain your
humble and devoted . . ." And so on.

THE CAPUCHIN
(Beaming)
I told you it was from a very worthy lord! I knew it could only concern some holy matter!

ROXANE
(To CHRISTIAN, *in an undertone)*
I read letters well, don't I?

CHRISTIAN
Hm!

ROXANE
(Loudly, with despair)
Oh! This is horrible!

THE CAPUCHIN
(Turning the light of his lantern on CYRANO*)*
Are you the . . .

CHRISTIAN
No, *I* am!

THE CAPUCHIN
(Turns the light on CHRISTIAN, *then, seeing how hand-some he is, appears to become suspicious.)*
But . . .

ROXANE
(Quickly, pretending to read again)
"P.S. You will make a gift of a thousand francs to the monastery."

THE CAPUCHIN
A worthy, worthy lord! *(To* ROXANE*)* Resign yourself!

ROXANE
(In a tone of martyrdom)
I am resigned. *(While* RAGUENEAU *opens the door for the* CAPUCHIN, *whom* CHRISTIAN *has invited to enter, she speaks softly to* CYRANO.*)* De Guiche will soon be here. Delay him, don't let him come in until . . .

CYRANO
I understand. *(To the* CAPUCHIN*)* How long will you need for the wedding ceremony?

THE CAPUCHIN

About a quarter of an hour.

CYRANO

(Pushing them all toward the house)
Hurry! I'll stay here.

ROXANE

(To CHRISTIAN*)*
Come!
(They go inside.)

Scene XII

Cyrano, alone.

CYRANO

How can I make De Guiche waste a quarter of an hour?
(Leaps onto the bench and climbs up the wall, toward the balcony.) Up we go! . . . I have my plan! *(The lutes begin playing a mournful melody.)* Aha! A man is coming! *(The tremolo becomes sinister.)* No doubt of it this time! *(He is now on the balcony. He pushes his hat down over his eyes, takes off his sword, wraps his cloak around himself, leans forward, and looks down.)* No, it's not too high. . . . *(He sits on the railing, takes one of the long tree branches that overhang the garden wall, pulls it toward him, and holds it with both hands, ready to swing down.)* I'm going to trouble this peaceful atmosphere a little!

Scene XIII

Cyrano, De Guiche.

DE GUICHE

(Entering masked, groping in the darkness)
What's happened to that cursed Capuchin?

CYRANO

My voice! What if he recognizes it? *(Lets go of the branch with one hand and makes the motion of turning an invisible key.)* There! I've unlocked my Gascon accent!

DE GUICHE

(Looking at the house)
Yes, this is it. I can hardly see where I'm going. This mask is so annoying! *(He walks toward the door.* CYRANO *leaps from the balcony, holding the branch, which bends and sets him down between* DE GUICHE *and the door. He pretends to fall heavily, as if from a great height, and lies motionless on the ground, as though dazed.* DE GUICHE *jumps back.)* What! . . . What's this? . . . *(He looks up, but the branch has already sprung back into place. Seeing nothing but the sky, he is mystified.)* Where did this man fall from?

CYRANO

(Sitting up, and speaking with a Gascon accent)
From the moon!

DE GUICHE

Did you say . . .

CYRANO

(Dreamily)
What time is it?

DE GUICHE

He's lost his reason!

CYRANO

What time is it? What country is this? What day? What season?

DE GUICHE

But . . .

CYRANO

I'm still dazed.

DE GUICHE

Sir . . .

CYRANO

I fell from the moon like a cannonball!

DE GUICHE

(Impatiently)
Look, sir . . .

CYRANO

(Loudly and emphatically, standing up)
I fell from the moon!

DE GUICHE

(Stepping back)
Very well, then, you fell from the moon! *(Aside)* He may be a maniac!

CYRANO

(Advancing toward him)
And I don't mean it metaphorically!

DE GUICHE

But . . .

CYRANO

A hundred years ago, or perhaps a minute ago—I have no idea how long my fall lasted—I was on that yellow sphere!

DE GUICHE

(Shrugging)
Yes, of course. Let me pass.

CYRANO

(Stepping in front of him)
Where am I? Be frank, don't hide anything from me! What is this place where I've just fallen like a meteorite?

DE GUICHE

Enough of this!

CYRANO

As I was falling, I wasn't able to choose my destination, and I don't know where I've landed. Has the weight of my posterior brought me back to earth, or to another moon?

DE GUICHE

Sir, I . . .

CYRANO

(With a cry of terror that makes DE GUICHE *step back again)*
Oh! My God! I see I've fallen into a country where people have black faces!

DE GUICHE

(Putting his hand to his face)
What . . .

CYRANO

(With a great show of fear)
Am I in Algiers? Are you a native?

DE GUICHE

(Who has felt his mask)
I'm wearing a mask.

CYRANO

(Pretending to be somewhat reassured)
Then am I in Venice, or Genoa?

DE GUICHE

(Trying to get past him)
A lady is expecting me. . . .

CYRANO

Ah, then I'm in Paris!

DE GUICHE

(Smiling in spite of himself)
This lunatic is rather amusing!

CYRANO

You're smiling?

DE GUICHE

Yes, but I still want you to let me pass!

CYRANO

(Beaming)
I've fallen back into Paris! *(Thoroughly at ease, smiling, brushing himself off, bowing)* Excuse me; I've just come by the latest whirlwind and I have ether all over me.

Such a journey! My eyes are full of stardust. I still have a little planet fur on my spurs. *(Picks something off his sleeve.)* A comet hair on my doublet! *(Pretends to blow it away.)*

DE GUICHE
(Beside himself with exasperation)

Sir! . . .
(Just as DE GUICHE *is about to pass,* CYRANO *stops him by putting out his leg, as though to show him something on it.)*

CYRANO

The Great Bear bit me as I passed. Look, you can see the tooth marks on my leg. Then, when I swerved to avoid Orion's Sword, I fell into the Scales. The pointer still marks my weight. *(Quickly prevents* DE GUICHE *from passing and takes hold of his doublet.)* If you were to squeeze my nose, sir, milk would spurt from it.

DE GUICHE

Milk?

CYRANO

From the Milky Way!

DE GUICHE

Oh! Stop this nonsense and let me . . .

CYRANO

Not yet. I haven't finished my story. *(Folds his arms.)* Would you believe me if I told you that during my fall I discovered that Sirius wears a nightcap? *(In a confidential tone)* The Little Bear is still too small to bite! *(Laughs.)* When I went through the Lyre, I broke one of its strings! *(Proudly)* But I intend to write a book* about all that. When I publish it, I'll take the stars I brought back in my cloak, at the risk of burning it, and use them for asterisks!

DE GUICHE

Sir, I've been very patient with you. Now will you please . . .

---

* The real Cyrano de Bergerac wrote a book describing a journey to the moon: *Histoire comique des Etats et Empires de la Lune.*

CYRANO

I understand. I'll be glad to oblige you.

DE GUICHE

At last!

CYRANO

You want me to tell you what the moon is like and whether anyone lives there, isn't that right?

DE GUICHE

No! No! I want to . . .

CYRANO

Yes, of course—you want to know how I got to the moon. I did it by a method that I invented myself.

DE GUICHE

(Discouraged)
He's raving mad!

CYRANO

(Disdainfully)
I didn't simply make a new version of Regiomontanus's*
stupid eagle or Archytas's timid dove.

DE GUICHE

He's a madman, but a learned madman.

CYRANO

No, I didn't imitate anything that had been done before!
(DE GUICHE succeeds in getting past him. He walks toward
ROXANE's *door while* CYRANO *follows him, ready to take*
hold of him.) I invented six ways to violate the virgin
sky!

DE GUICHE

(Stopping and turning around)
Six?

CYRANO

(Volubly)
I could have clothed my naked body with crystal bottles

* Regiomontanus (1436–76, real name Johann Müller), German
mathematician and astronomer who is said to have made a mechanical bird capable of flying.

full of dew and exposed myself to the morning sun; then, as the sun drew up the dew, I would have been drawn up with it!

DE GUICHE
(Surprised, and taking a step toward CYRANO)
Yes, that's one way!

CYRANO
(Stepping back to lead him away from the door)
And I could have rarefied the air in a cedar chest by means of twenty burning-mirrors* suitably arranged, thus producing a great rush of wind that would have sent me on my way!

DE GUICHE
(Taking another step toward him)
Two!

CYRANO
(Still moving back)
Or, with my mechanical skill and my knowledge of pyrotechnics, I could have constructed a large steel grasshopper propelled by successive explosions of gunpowder, and ridden it into the blue realm of the stars!

DE GUICHE
(Following him without realizing it, and counting on his fingers)
Three!

CYRANO
Since smoke tends to rise, I could have blown enough of it into a globe to carry me away!

DE GUICHE
(Increasingly surprised, and still following him)
Four!

CYRANO
Since the new moon likes to suck up the marrow of cattle, I could have coated my body with it!

---

* A burning-mirror is a concave mirror used for producing intense heat by concentrating the sun's rays.

DE GUICHE

(Fascinated)

Five!

CYRANO

*(Who, while speaking, has led him to the other side
of the square, near a bench)*

Finally, I could have sat on a sheet of iron and thrown
a magnet into the air. It's a very good method: the iron
follows the magnet in its flight, then you quickly throw
the magnet again, and keep repeating the process until
you've reached the moon!

DE GUICHE

Six! . . . But which of those six excellent methods did
you choose?

CYRANO

A seventh!

DE GUICHE

Amazing! Tell me about it.

CYRANO

Try to guess.

DE GUICHE

This rascal is becoming interesting!

CYRANO

*(Making a sound of waves, with broad, mysterious
gestures)*

Hoo! . . . Hoo! . . .

DE GUICHE

What's that?

CYRANO

Can't you guess?

DE GUICHE

No!

CYRANO

The tide! . . . After taking a dip in the sea, I lay on the
beach at the hour when the moon was exerting the pull
that causes the tides, and I was lifted into the air—head-

first, of course, since it was my hair that held the most moisture. I was rising straight up, slowly and effortlessly, like an angel, when suddenly I felt a shock! Then . . .

DE GUICHE
(Sitting down on the bench, seized with curiosity)
Yes? Then what?

CYRANO
Then . . . *(Resumes his natural voice.)* The quarter of an hour has passed, so I won't keep you any longer. The wedding is over.

DE GUICHE
(Leaping to his feet)
I must be losing my mind! That voice! . . . *(The door of the house opens. LACKEYS appear, carrying lighted candelabra. The stage lighting becomes brighter. CYRANO takes off his hat, whose brim has remained turned down throughout the scene.)* And that nose! . . . Cyrano!

CYRANO
(Bowing)
At your service. They've just been married.

DE GUICHE
Who? *(He turns around. Tableau. Behind the LACKEYS, ROXANE and CHRISTIAN are holding hands. The CAPUCHIN follows them, smiling. RAGUENEAU is also holding a candelabrum. The DUENNA brings up the rear, looking bewildered and wearing a dressing gown.)* Good God!

Scene XIV

Cyrano, De Guiche, Roxane, Christian, the Capuchin, Ragueneau, Lackeys, the Duenna.

DE GUICHE
(To ROXANE)
You! *(With amazement, recognizing CHRISTIAN)* And he? . . . *(Bowing to ROXANE with admiration)* I congratulate you on your cleverness! *(To CYRANO)* And to you, the great inventor, my compliments! Your story would

have stopped a saint at the gates of heaven! Write down the details of it, because you really could use them in a book!

CYRANO
(Bowing)
I promise to follow your advice.

THE CAPUCHIN
(Showing the two lovers to DE GUICHE *and nodding his white-bearded head with satisfaction)*
Here's the handsome couple you've united, my son!

DE GUICHE
(Giving him an icy look)
Yes. *(To* ROXANE*)* And now you must tell your husband good-by, madame.

ROXANE
Why?

DE GUICHE
(To CHRISTIAN*)*
The regiment is about to leave. Join it!

ROXANE
To go to war?

DE GUICHE
Of course!

ROXANE
But the Cadets aren't going!

DE GUICHE
Yes, they are. *(Takes the envelope from his pocket.)* Here's the order. *(To* CHRISTIAN*)* Deliver it at once, Baron.

ROXANE
(Throwing herself in CHRISTIAN'*s arms)*
Christian!

DE GUICHE
(Sneering, to CYRANO*)*
The wedding night is still a long way off!

CYRANO
(Aside)
He thinks that's bitter news to me!

CHRISTIAN
(To ROXANE*)*
Oh! Kiss me again!

CYRANO
Come, come, enough!

CHRISTIAN
(Continuing to kiss ROXANE*)*
It's hard to leave her. . . . You can't know. . . .

CYRANO
(Trying to lead him away)
I do know. . . .
(Drums are heard beating in the distance.)

DE GUICHE
(Who has gone upstage)
The regiment! It's leaving!

ROXANE
(To CYRANO, *clutching* CHRISTIAN, *whom he is still trying to lead away)*
I trust you to look after him! Promise me that nothing will endanger his life!

CYRANO
I'll do my best, but I can't promise anything.

ROXANE
(Still holding CHRISTIAN *back)*
Promise me that you'll make him be very careful!

CYRANO
I'll try, but . . .

ROXANE
(Still holding CHRISTIAN*)*
Promise me that he'll never be cold during that terrible siege!

CYRANO
I'll do whatever I can, but . . .

ROXANE

(Still holding CHRISTIAN*)*
Promise me that he'll be faithful!

CYRANO

Of course he will! But . . .

ROXANE

(Still holding CHRISTIAN*)*
Promise me that he'll write often!

CYRANO

(Stopping)
Ah! That's one thing I can promise you!

CURTAIN

Act Four

✥

The Gascon Cadets

The post occupied by CARBON DE CASTEL-JALOUX's *company in the siege of Arras.*

In the background, an embankment crossing the entire stage. Beyond, a plain covered with siegeworks. Far off in the distance, the walls and rooftops of Arras are silhouetted against the sky.

Tents, scattered weapons, drums, etc. Daybreak is near. Yellowish glow in the east. Sentries at intervals. Campfires.

Wrapped in their cloaks, the GASCON CADETS *are asleep.* CARBON *and* LE BRET *are awake. They are both pale and gaunt.* CHRISTIAN, *sleeping like the others, is in the foreground, with the light of a campfire on his face. Silence.*

Scene I

Christian, Carbon de Castel-Jaloux, Le Bret, the Cadets, then Cyrano.

LE BRET

It's horrible!

CARBON

Yes. Not one scrap of food left.

LE BRET

Mordious!

CARBON
(Motioning him to speak more softly)
Do your swearing in a whisper! You'll wake them up!
(To the CADETS*)* Sh! Sleep! *(To* LE BRET*)* As the proverb
says, he who sleeps dines.

LE BRET

Yes, but that's not much comfort when you have insom-
nia! What a famine!
(A few shots are heard in the distance.)

CARBON

Damn those shots! They'll wake my children! *(To the*
CADETS, *who have begun to raise their heads)* Go back
to sleep!
(The CADETS *settle down again, then there are more
shots, from closer range.)*

A CADET
(Stirring)
What, again?

CARBON

It's nothing, only Cyrano coming back.
(The heads that have been raised are lowered again.)

A SENTRY
(Offstage)
Halt! Who goes there?

CYRANO'S VOICE

Bergerac!

THE SENTRY ON THE PARAPET

Halt! Who goes there?

CYRANO

(Appearing on the parapet)
Bergerac, you idiot!
(Comes down from the parapet. LE BRET *anxiously goes forward to meet him.)*

LE BRET

Thank God you're back!

CYRANO

(Motioning him not to awaken anyone)
Sh!

LE BRET

Are you wounded?

CYRANO

You know very well that they make it a habit to miss me every morning!

LE BRET

Don't you think it's going a little too far to risk your life every day to send a letter?

CYRANO

(Stopping in front of CHRISTIAN*)*
I promised he would write often! *(Looks at him.)* He's asleep. His face is pale. If poor Roxane knew he was dying of hunger . . . But he's still handsome!

LE BRET

Hurry, go and get some sleep!

CYRANO

Don't nag me, Le Bret! And don't worry: I always cross the Spanish lines at a place where I know the soldiers get drunk every night.

LE BRET

You ought to bring us some food.

CYRANO

I have to travel light to get through! . . . But you can expect a change by this evening. If I saw what I think I saw, the French will soon either eat or die.

LE BRET

Tell me about it!

CYRANO

No, I'm not sure. . . . You'll see!

CARBON

We're the besiegers, and yet we're starving! It's shameful!

LE BRET

Unfortunately, nothing could be more complicated than this siege. We're besieging Arras, we ourselves are caught in a trap, the Cardinal Prince of Spain is besieging us. . . .

CYRANO

Someone ought to come and besiege *him*.

LE BRET

Excuse me if I don't laugh.

CYRANO

You're excused.

LE BRET

To think that every day you risk a life like yours to carry . . . (*Sees* CYRANO *walking toward a tent.*) Where are you going?

CYRANO

I'm going to write another one.
   (*Lifts the flap of the tent and disappears.*)

Scene II

The same, without Cyrano.

   (*Daylight is advancing; the pink glow of dawn has appeared. The town of Arras is illuminated on the horizon. From the left, a distant cannon shot is heard, immediately followed by a drumbeat. Other drums begin beating, nearer. The drumbeats answer each other, draw closer, are heard almost on the stage, and finally fade away to the right, crossing the camp. Sounds of awakening. Officers' voices in the distance.)*

CARBON

(With a sigh)
Reveille, alas! *(The* CADETS *stir in their cloaks and stretch.)* Their delicious sleep has ended, and I know only too well what their first words will be!

A CADET

(Sitting up)
I'm hungry!

ANOTHER

I'm starving!

ALL

Oh! . . .

CARBON

On your feet, all of you!

THIRD CADET

I can't stand up!

FOURTH CADET

I can't move!

FIRST CADET

(Looking at himself in a piece of polished armor)
My tongue is yellow—living on air has given me indigestion!

FIFTH CADET

I'd give my baron's coronet for a bite of cheese!

SIXTH CADET

If I don't get something to keep the walls of my stomach from growing together, I'll withdraw to my tent, like Achilles!

SEVENTH CADET

Yes! We must have food!

CARBON

(Calling softly into the tent where CYRANO *has gone)*
Cyrano!

OTHER CADETS

We're dying!

CARBON
(Still softly, standing at the doorway of the tent)
I need your help! You always know how to answer
them—come and cheer them up!

SECOND CADET
(Hurrying to the FIRST CADET, *who is chewing some-
thing)*
What are you eating?

FIRST CADET
Ammunition wadding cooked in axle grease, using a
steel helmet as a pot. There's not much game in this
country!

ANOTHER CADET
(Entering)
I've just been hunting!

ANOTHER
(Entering)
I've been fishing in the river!

ALL
*(Standing up and rushing toward the two new-
comers)*
What?—What have you brought?—A pheasant?—A
carp?—Show us!

THE FISHERMAN

A gudgeon!

THE HUNTER

A sparrow!

ALL
(Exasperated)
Enough!—Let's mutiny!

CARBON
Cyrano! Help!
(It is now broad daylight.)

Scene III

The same, with Cyrano.

CYRANO

(Calmly coming out of the tent with a quill pen behind his ear and a book in his hand)
What's the trouble? *(Silence. He speaks to the* FIRST
CADET.*)* Why are you standing so stiffly?

FIRST CADET

I have to.

CYRANO

Why?

FIRST CADET

My stomach is so empty that if I bend at the waist I'll
break in half!

CYRANO

Be glad you've lost weight: it may save your life.

FIRST CADET

How?

CYRANO

By making you a smaller target for the enemy!

SECOND CADET

I'm so hungry I could eat a whole side of beef!

CYRANO

Now there's a meaty remark!

THIRD CADET

My belly is hollow!

CYRANO

We'll use it for a drum.

FOURTH CADET

You must be as hungry as we are. How do you stand it?

CYRANO

I think of how long it's been since the last time I ate,
and that makes me so sad I lose my appetite.

FIFTH CADET

I don't think about my last meal, I worry about my next one!

CYRANO

That's good. Maybe you'll worry yourself into a stew.

SIXTH CADET

There's nothing to relieve our hunger, nothing!

CYRANO

(Tossing him the book he has been holding in his hand)

Here, read the *Iliad:* it will give you food for thought.

SEVENTH CADET

In Paris, Cardinal Richelieu eats his fill!

CYRANO

Do you think he ought to send you a partridge?

SEVENTH CADET

Why not? And some wine to go with it!

CYRANO

I'll have Burgundy, please.

SEVENTH CADET

I'm sure Richelieu will be glad to send you some from his own cellar.

CYRANO

Of course—generosity is one of his cardinal virtues.

EIGHTH CADET

Why is it that *you* never complain about your hunger?

CYRANO

Because there's one thing I'm not hungry enough to swallow: my pride.

FIRST CADET

(Shrugging)

You're never at a loss for a clever remark.

CYRANO

Yes, and I hope that when death comes to me it will find me fighting in a good cause and making a clever remark! I want to be struck down by the only noble weapon, the sword, wielded by an adversary worthy of me, and to die not in a sickbed but on the field of glory, with sharp steel in my heart and a flash of wit on my lips!

ALL THE CADETS

(Shouting)
I'm hungry!

CYRANO

(Folding his arms)
Can't you think of anything but food? . . . Come here, Bertrandou. You're a fifer now, but you were once a shepherd; take out your fife and play some of the old Gascon music for these gluttons! Let them hear those soft, haunting melodies in which each note is like a little sister, melodies that hold the sound of loved voices and have the slowness of smoke rising from the chimneys of our home villages, melodies that speak to us in our mother tongue! *(BERTRANDOU, the old fifer, sits down and prepares his fife.)* Your fife is now a sorrowful warrior, but while your fingers move over it like birds dancing a minuet, let it remember that before it was made of ebony it was a simple reed! Let it marvel at its own song and recognize in it the soul of its rustic, peaceful youth! *(BERTRANDOU begins playing melodies from the south of France.)* Listen, Gascons. . . . He's no longer playing the martial fife: it's now the flute of our forests! It's not a call to battle, but the slow piping of our goatherds! Listen. . . . It's our valleys, our moors, our woodlands; it's a dark-haired little cowherd wearing a red beret; it's the sweetness of evenings on the banks of the Dordogne. . . . Listen, Gascons: it's all of Gascony!
(The CADETS have all sat down and dreamily bowed their heads. Now and then one of them furtively wipes away a tear with his sleeve or his cloak.)

CARBON

(Softly, to CYRANO)
You're making them weep!

CYRANO

Yes, from homesickness! It's a nobler pain than hunger.

I'm glad that their suffering has shifted from their bellies to their hearts.

CARBON

You'll weaken them by stirring up such feelings!

CYRANO
(Motioning the drummer to approach)

Not at all! The courage in their blood is easily awakened. It takes only . . .
(He makes a gesture and the drummer beats a roll.)

ALL THE CADETS
(Leaping to their feet and rushing for their weapons)

What?—Where?—What is it?

CYRANO
(Smiling)

You see? It takes only a drumbeat! Farewell dreams, regrets, homesickness, memories of love! What the fife brought, the drum has taken away!

A CADET
(Looking upstage)

Oh! Here comes Monsieur de Guiche!
(The CADETS all murmur irritably.)

CYRANO
(Smiling)

That's a flattering greeting!

THE CADET

He annoys us!

SECOND CADET

He's coming to strut in front of us with his big lace collar over his armor!

THIRD CADET

A soldier shouldn't wear cloth over steel!

FIRST CADET

Not unless he has a boil on his neck!

SECOND CADET

He's not a soldier, he's a courtier!

FOURTH CADET

He's his uncle's nephew!

CARBON

He's still a Gascon.

FIRST CADET

Not a real one! A real Gascon is mad, and he's not.
Don't trust him, because there's nothing more dangerous
than a sane Gascon!

LE BRET

He looks pale.

FIFTH CADET

He's hungry, like the rest of us poor devils, but since his
armor has gilded studs, his stomach cramps glitter in
the sunlight!

CYRANO

(Urgently)
We mustn't let him see us looking miserable! Take out
your cards, your pipes, your dice. . . . *(They all quickly
begin playing cards and dice on drums, stools, and their
cloaks spread out on the ground, and they light their long
pipes.)* As for me, I'm going to read Descartes.
*(He walks slowly back and forth, reading from a
small book that he has taken from his pocket. Tableau.* DE GUICHE *enters. The* CADETS *all seem happily
absorbed in what they are doing.* DE GUICHE *is very
pale. He walks toward* CARBON.*)*

Scene IV

The same, with De Guiche.

DE GUICHE

(To CARBON*)*
Ah! Good morning! *(Aside, with satisfaction, after they
have observed each other a moment)* He looks green
around the gills!

CARBON
(Aside, also with satisfaction)
His eyes are sunken, and big as saucers!

DE GUICHE
(Looking at the CADETS*)*
So here are the grumblers! . . . Yes, gentlemen, it's been
reported to me from all sides that you jeer at me, that
you mountain aristocrats, you country gentlemen, you
rustic barons, have nothing but contempt for your colonel. You call me a schemer and a courtier, it upsets you
to see a lace collar on my armor, and you're constantly
expressing indignation at the idea that a man can be a
Gascon without being a ragged pauper! *(Silence. The*
CADETS *continue their games and smoking.)* Am I going
to have you punished by your captain? No.

CARBON
Let me point out to you that I'm free to do as I see fit,
and I don't choose to punish my men.

DE GUICHE
Oh?

CARBON
I've paid for my company; it's my own. I obey only battle orders.

DE GUICHE
That will do! *(To the* CADETS*)* I can afford to despise
your mockery, because my conduct under fire is well
known. Only yesterday, at Bapaume, I furiously drove
back Count de Bucquoi. Bringing my men down upon
his like an avalanche, I charged three times!

CYRANO
(Without looking up from his book)
And don't forget your white scarf.

DE GUICHE
(Surprised and pleased)
Ah, you know about that? . . . Yes, as I was rallying my
men for the third charge, I was caught in a rush of fugi-
tives and swept along toward the enemy. I was in danger
of being captured or shot when I had the good sense to

take off the scarf that showed my rank and drop it on the ground. I was thus able to slip away from the Spaniards without attracting attention, then come back to them, followed by all my men, and beat them! . . . Well, what do you think of that?
(The CADETS *do not seem to have been listening, but they now stop puffing on their pipes and suspend the movements of their card and dice games; they are waiting.)*

CYRANO

I think that Henry the Fourth would never have given up his white plume,* even when surrounded by the enemy.
(Silent joy among the CADETS. *They resume laying down their cards, rolling their dice, and smoking their pipes.)*

DE GUICHE

But my trick succeeded!
(The CADETS *again become motionless, waiting.)*

CYRANO

Perhaps, but I don't believe in declining the honor of being a target. *(The* CADETS *resume their activities with growing satisfaction.)* You and I, sir, have different ideas of courage. If I had been there when you dropped the scarf, I would have picked it up and put it on.

DE GUICHE

That's nothing but Gascon bragging!

CYRANO

Bragging? Lend me the scarf and accept my offer to wear it while I lead an assault today.

DE GUICHE

And that's a Gascon offer! You know very well that my scarf remained on the riverbank, in a place that's now under heavy enemy fire, so that no one can go and bring it back.

---

* Before the Battle of Ivry, in 1590, Henry IV said to his soldiers, "If you lose your banners, rally around my white plume. You will always find it on the path of honor and glory."

CYRANO
(Taking the white scarf from his pocket and holding it out to DE GUICHE)
Here it is.
(Silence. The CADETS *stifle their laughter behind their cards and dice cups.* DE GUICHE *turns around and looks at them. They immediately take on serious expressions and resume their games. One of them casually whistles a melody played earlier by the fifer.)*

DE GUICHE
(Taking the scarf)
Thank you. Now that I have this piece of white cloth, I can use it for a signal that I was hesitating to make.
(Climbs to the top of the embankment and waves the scarf several times.)

ALL THE CADETS
What! . . .

THE SENTINEL ON THE PARAPET
I see a man down there, running away!

DE GUICHE
(Returning)
He's a false Spanish spy. He's very useful to me. He reports to the enemy whatever I tell him, which makes it possible for us to influence their decisions.

CYRANO
He's contemptible!

DE GUICHE
(Nonchalantly tying his scarf around his neck)
He's valuable. Now, what was I saying? . . . Ah, yes, I was about to tell you some news. Last night, in a supreme effort to get food for us, the Marshal quietly left for Dourlens, where our supplies are. He'll arrive there by traveling across the fields, but in order to come back safely he took so many troops with him that we're now extremely vulnerable to an enemy attack: half the army is absent!

CARBON
If the Spaniards knew that . . . But they don't, do they?

DE GUICHE

Yes, they know. And they're going to attack.

CARBON

Ah!

DE GUICHE

My false spy came to warn me. He said, "I can make the attack come at any place you like, by reporting that it's your most weakly defended point. Just tell me where." I answered, "Very well, leave the camp and watch our lines. I'll signal to you from the place I've chosen."

CARBON

(To the CADETS*)*
Gentlemen, prepare yourselves.
(They all stand up. Sounds of swords and sword belts being buckled on.)

DE GUICHE

The attack will begin in an hour.

FIRST CADET

Oh. . . . In that case . . .
(They all sit down again and resume their games.)

DE GUICHE

(To CARBON*)*
The most important thing is to gain time. The Marshal will soon be on his way back.

CARBON

And how shall we gain time?

DE GUICHE

You will be so kind as to fight till the last of you is killed.

CYRANO

Ah, so that's your revenge?

DE GUICHE

I won't pretend that if I liked you I would have chosen you and your men, but since you're known to be incomparably brave, I'm serving my king by serving my rancor.

CYRANO

(Bowing)
Allow me to be grateful to you, sir.

DE GUICHE

(Returning his bow)
I know that you like to fight against odds of a hundred
to one. I'm sure this is an opportunity you wouldn't have
wanted to miss.
(Goes upstage with CARBON*)*

CYRANO

(To the CADETS*)*
Gentlemen, your Gascon coat of arms bears six chev-
rons, blue and gold. We're about to add one more, of a
different color: bloodred!
*(*DE GUICHE *is talking quietly with* CARBON *in the
background. Orders are being given. Preparations to
meet the attack are being made.* CYRANO *goes to*
CHRISTIAN, *who is standing motionless, with his arms
folded.)*

CYRANO

(Putting his hand on CHRISTIAN's *shoulder)*
Christian?

CHRISTIAN

(Shaking his head)
Roxane. . . .

CYRANO

Yes, I know. . . .

CHRISTIAN

I wish I could at least pour out my heart to her in one
last letter.

CYRANO

I thought something might happen today, so . . . *(Takes
a letter from his doublet.)* . . . I wrote your farewell.

CHRISTIAN

Let me see!

CYRANO

Do you want . . .

CHRISTIAN

(Taking the letter)
Of course! *(Opens it and begins reading it, then stops.)*
What's this?

CYRANO

Where?

CHRISTIAN

Here—this little stain.

CYRANO

(Quickly takes the letter back and looks at it with an innocent expression.)
A stain?

CHRISTIAN

It was made by a tear!

CYRANO

Yes. . . . A poet is sometimes caught up in his own game; that's what makes it so fascinating. This letter, you understand . . . It was so moving that I made myself weep while I was writing it.

CHRISTIAN

Weep?

CYRANO

Yes, because . . . Dying is no great matter. What's unbearable is the thought of never seeing her again. And it's true: I'll never see her . . . (CHRISTIAN *looks at him.*) . . . we'll never . . . *(Quickly)* . . . you'll never . . .

CHRISTIAN

(Snatching the letter from him)
Give me that letter!
(A distant clamor is heard from the edge of the camp.)

SENTRY'S VOICE

My God! Who can that be?
(Shots, shouts, jingling of harness bells)

CARBON

What is it?

THE SENTRY
(Now on the parapet)
A carriage!
(Everyone rushes to look)

VOICES
What!—In the camp?—It's coming this way!—It seems
to have come from the direction of the enemy!—The
enemy?—Shoot!—No! Didn't you hear what the driver
shouted?—What was it?—He said, "King's service!"
*(Everyone is now on the parapet, looking down. The
sound of the jingling bells is coming closer.)*

DE GUICHE
King's service?
(The men all come down and fall into line.)

CARBON
Hats off, everyone!

DE GUICHE
(Shouting into the wings)
King's service! . . . Line up, you rabble! Don't you know
how to receive a carriage in the king's service?
*(The carriage enters at a rapid trot. It is covered with
mud and dust. The curtains are drawn. Two* FOOT-
MEN *behind. It stops abruptly.)*

CARBON
(Shouting)
Beat the general salute!
(Ruffle of drums. All the CADETS *take off their hats.)*

DE GUICHE
Lower the step!
(Two men rush forward. The carriage door opens.)

ROXANE
(Alighting from the carriage)
Good morning!
*(The men have bowed low; hearing the sound of a
woman's voice, they all straighten up at once. Stupe-
faction.)*

Scene V

The same, with Roxane.

DE GUICHE

King's service? You?

ROXANE

I'm in the service of the greatest of all kings: love!

CYRANO

Oh! My God!

CHRISTIAN
(Hurrying to her)
You! Why?

ROXANE

This siege had lasted too long!

CHRISTIAN

Why . . .

ROXANE

I'll tell you!

CYRANO
*(Who, at the sound of her voice, has remained rooted
to the spot, not daring to turn his eyes toward her)*
I can't look at her. . . .

DE GUICHE

You can't stay here!

ROXANE
(Gaily)
Yes I can! Would you please bring me a drum to sit on?
(Sits on the drum that is brought for her.) Thank you!
(Laughs.) They shot at my carriage! *(Proudly)* We met
a patrol! . . . It looks as if it had been made from a
pumpkin, like the carriage in the fairy tale, doesn't it?
And my footmen look as if they had once been rats.
(Throws a kiss to CHRISTIAN.) Good morning! *(Looks at
everyone.)* You don't seem very cheerful! . . . Did you
know that Arras is a long way from Paris? *(Notices* CY-
RANO.) Cousin! Delighted to see you!

CYRANO

(Approaching)
And I'm amazed! How . . .

ROXANE

How did I find the army? It was quite simple: I went
where I saw that the countryside had been laid waste.
Oh, such horrors! I would never have believed them if
I hadn't seen them! Gentlemen, if that's how you serve
your king, I much prefer to serve mine!

CYRANO

This is insane! How the devil did you get here?

ROXANE

I went through the Spanish lines.

FIRST CADET

Trust a woman to do a thing like that!

DE GUICHE

How were you able to pass?

LE BRET

It must have been very difficult!

ROXANE

Not very. I simply rolled along in my carriage. Whenever
a Spanish officer gave me a suspicious look, I smiled at
him sweetly from the window, and since, with all due
deference to the French, Spaniards are the most gallant
gentlemen in the world, I was always allowed to continue on my way.

CARBON

I'm sure your smile is a passport that would let you go
anywhere! But you must have been asked to say where
you were going.

ROXANE

Yes, often. I always answered, "I'm going to see my
lover." No matter how fierce he had looked before, the
Spanish officer would solemnly close the door of my carriage, and with a gesture that any king would have en-
vied, wave away the muskets that had already been
aimed at me. Then, superbly gracious and proud, with

his spurs thrusting out beneath his lace and the plume of his hat floating in the breeze, he would bow and say, "Pass, Señorita!"

CHRISTIAN

But Roxane . . .

ROXANE

Yes, I said "my lover"—forgive me! But don't you understand that if I'd said "my husband," no one would have let me pass?

CHRISTIAN

But . . .

ROXANE

What's the matter?

DE GUICHE

You must leave here!

ROXANE

Leave?

CYRANO

Yes, and quickly!

LE BRET

Immediately!

CHRISTIAN

Yes!

ROXANE

But why?

CHRISTIAN

(Embarrassed)
Because . . .

CYRANO

(Embarrassed)
In three-quarters of an hour . . .

DE GUICHE

(Embarrassed)
Or maybe an hour . . .

CARBON

(Embarrassed)
You'd better . . .

LE BRET

(Embarrassed)
You might . . .

ROXANE

I'm staying. There's going to be a battle, isn't there?

ALL

Oh, no!

ROXANE

He's my husband! *(Throws herself into* CHRISTIAN*'s arms.)* Let them kill me with you!

CHRISTIAN

Such a look in your eyes!

ROXANE

Do I have to tell you why?

DE GUICHE

(Desperately)
This is a terribly dangerous post!

ROXANE

(Turning around)
Dangerous?

CYRANO

He knows what he's saying: he gave it to us!

ROXANE

(To DE GUICHE*)*
Ah, so you wanted to make me a widow!

DE GUICHE

Oh! I swear to you that . . .

ROXANE

No! I don't care what happens to me now! I'm staying! Besides, it's amusing.

CYRANO

What? You're both an intellectual and a heroine?

ROXANE

I'm your cousin, Monsieur de Bergerac.

A CADET

We'll defend you!

ROXANE
(More and more excited)
I believe it, my friends!

SECOND CADET
(Ecstatically)
The whole camp smells of iris!

ROXANE

And I'm wearing a hat that will look good in the battle! . . . *(Looks at DE GUICHE.)* Don't you think it's time for you to leave? The fighting may begin. . . .

DE GUICHE

This is too much! I'm going to inspect my cannons, and then I'll come back. . . . You still have time: change your mind!

ROXANE

Never!
(DE GUICHE leaves.)

Scene VI

The same, without De Guiche.

CHRISTIAN
(Beseechingly)
Roxane! . . .

ROXANE

No!

FIRST CADET
(To the others)
She's staying!

ALL

(Jostling one another as they hurry to make themselves more presentable)

A comb!—Soap!—Give me a needle, I have to sew up a hole!—A ribbon!—Your mirror!—My cuffs!—Your mustache curler!—A razor!

ROXANE

(To CYRANO, who is again pleading with her)

No! Nothing will make me leave this place!

(CARBON, like the others, has tightened his buckles, dusted himself off, brushed his hat, straightened his plume, and put on his cuffs. He now approaches ROXANE.)

CARBON

(Ceremoniously, to ROXANE)

That being the case, perhaps it would be fitting for me to introduce some of the gentlemen who will have the honor of dying before your eyes. *(ROXANE bows and waits, holding CHRISTIAN's arm. CARBON begins making the introductions.)* Baron de Peyrescous de Colignac.

THE CADET

(Bowing)

Madame. . . .

CARBON

Baron de Casterac de Cahuzac . . . Vidame de Malgouyre Estressac Lésbas d'Escarabiot . . . Chevalier d'Antignac-Juzet . . . Baron Hillot de Blagnac-Saléchan de Castel-Crabioules . . .

ROXANE

Do you all have such long names?

BARON HILLOT

Yes, every one of us!

CARBON

(To ROXANE)

Open the hand that holds your handkerchief.

ROXANE

(Opens her hand and the handkerchief falls.)

Why?

(The whole company makes a move to pick it up.)

CARBON
(Quickly picking it up)
My company had no flag, but now it has the finest one in the whole army!

ROXANE
(Smiling)
It's rather small.

CARBON
(Tying the handkerchief to his lance)
But it's trimmed with lace!

A CADET
(To the others)
Now that I've seen her face, I could die without regret if I only had a little food in my stomach!

CARBON
(Indignantly, having overheard)
Shame! Speaking of food when an exquisite lady . . .

ROXANE
But I'm hungry too! It must be the cool air. I'd like some pâté, cold chicken, and wine. Would you please bring it to me?
(Consternation)

A CADET
Bring it to you?

ANOTHER
Where the devil can we get it?

ROXANE
(Calmly)
In my carriage.

ALL
What!

ROXANE
But the food will have to be carved and served. Look at my coachman a little more closely, gentlemen, and you'll recognize a valuable man. If you like, each sauce will be reheated.

THE CADETS
(Rushing toward the carriage)
It's Ragueneau!
(Loud cheers)

ROXANE
(Watching them)
Poor men! . . .

CYRANO
(Kissing her hand)
You're our fairy godmother!

RAGUENEAU
*(Standing on the driver's seat like a mountebank in
a public square)*
Gentlemen! . . .
(Outburst of enthusiasm)

THE CADETS
Bravo! Bravo!

RAGUENEAU
The Spaniards were so busy feasting their eyes that they
didn't eye the feast!
(Applause)

CYRANO
(Softly, to CHRISTIAN*)*
Christian!

RAGUENEAU
Distracted by Beauty, they overlooked . . . *(Picks up
a roast suckling pig on a tray and holds it aloft.)* . . .
the Beast!
(Applause. The tray is passed from hand to hand.)

CYRANO
(Softly, to CHRISTIAN*)*
Please let me have a word with you.

RAGUENEAU
The sight they saw was so pleasant that they failed to
notice . . . *(Picks up another tray.)* . . . this pheasant!
*(More enthusiasm. The tray is seized by a dozen
eager hands.)*

CYRANO
(Softly, to CHRISTIAN*)*
I want to talk to you!

ROXANE
(To the CADETS *who are coming downstage, their arms laden with food)*
Set it down on the ground! *(Aided by the two imperturbable* FOOTMEN, *she begins making preparations for a picnic; then she speaks to* CHRISTIAN *just as* CYRANO *is about to take him aside.)* Come here and make yourself useful!
*(*CHRISTIAN *goes to help her.* CYRANO *shows signs of anxiety.)*

RAGUENEAU
A peacock with truffles!

FIRST CADET
(Coming downstage with a blissful expression, carving himself a thick slice of ham)
It will be easier to face death when we've stuffed our guts! *(Embarrassed, seeing* ROXANE*)* Excuse me, I mean when we've had a good meal.

RAGUENEAU
(Throwing out the cushions of the carriage)
The cushions are full of quail!
(Tumult. The cushions are ripped open. Joyous laughter.)

THIRD CADET
Hallelujah!

RAGUENEAU
(Throwing out bottles)
Wine! Ruby red and tawny white!

ROXANE
(Tossing a folded tablecloth to CYRANO*)*
Here, spread this tablecloth! It's time you did your share of the work!

RAGUENEAU
(Brandishing a lantern that he has taken from the carriage)
Each lantern is a little pantry!

CYRANO

(Softly, to CHRISTIAN, *while they spread the table-cloth together)*
I must talk to you before you talk to her!

RAGUENEAU

(More and more exuberant)
The handle of my whip is a sausage!

ROXANE

(Pouring wine and handing out food)
Since we're the ones who are going to be killed, we don't care about the rest of the army! Everything for the Gascons! And if De Guiche comes, he's not invited! *(Going from one to another)* There's plenty of time. . . . Don't eat so fast! . . . Drink a little wine. . . . Why are you weeping?

FIRST CADET

It's too good!

ROXANE

Sh! . . . Red or white? . . . Bring some bread for Monsieur de Carbon! . . . A knife! . . . Hand me your plate. . . . Would you like some of the crust? . . . I'll serve you! . . . Burgundy? . . . A wing?

CYRANO

(Following her, laden with dishes, helping her serve)
She's adorable!

ROXANE

(Going to CHRISTIAN)
And what would *you* like?

CHRISTIAN

Nothing.

ROXANE

That won't do! At least take a biscuit dipped in muscatel.

CHRISTIAN

(Trying to hold her back)
Tell me why you came.

ROXANE

Later. For now, my time belongs to these poor men.

LE BRET

*(Who has gone upstage to pass a loaf of bread, at
the end of a lance, to the* SENTRY ON THE PARAPET*)*
Here comes De Guiche!

CYRANO

Quickly! Hide the food, the bottles, the baskets, everything! And act as if nothing had happened! *(To* RA-
GUENEAU*)* Hurry back to your driver's seat! . . . Is
everything out of sight?
*(In the twinkling of an eye, everything is hidden in
the tents or under cloaks and hats.* DE GUICHE *enters
rapidly, then suddenly stops, sniffing. Silence.)*

Scene VII

The same, with De Guiche.

DE GUICHE

Something smells good here.

A CADET

(Casually singing)
Tra-la-la . . .

DE GUICHE

(Looking at him)
What's the matter with you? Your face is red.

THE CADET

It's nothing. We'll soon be fighting, and the thought of
it has made the blood rush to my head.

SECOND CADET

Poom-poom-poom . . .

DE GUICHE

(Turning around)
What's that?

SECOND CADET
(Slightly drunk)
Nothing. Just a song, a little song. . . .

DE GUICHE
You're in a gay mood!

SECOND CADET
It's because danger is approaching!

DE GUICHE
(Calling CARBON, *to give an order)*
Captain! I . . . *(Stops short when he sees him.)* You too!
You look happy as a lark!

CARBON
*(His face crimson, making an evasive gesture while
hiding a bottle of wine behind his back)*
Well, I . . .

DE GUICHE
I had one cannon left over. I had it brought there . . .
(Points offstage.) . . . in that corner. Your men can use
it if they need it.

A CADET
(With affectation)
How thoughtful of you!

SECOND CADET
(Smiling graciously)
We're deeply grateful for your concern!

DE GUICHE
You're both mad! . . . *(Curtly)* Since you're not used to
cannons, I must warn you not to stand behind this one
when it recoils.

FIRST CADET
Oh, pfft!

DE GUICHE
(Going to him, furious)
Look here! . . .

FIRST CADET
A Gascon's gun never moves to the rear!

DE GUICHE
(Taking him by the arm and shaking him)
You're drunk! . . . But on what?

FIRST CADET
(Loftily)
The smell of gunpowder!
(DE GUICHE shrugs, pushes him away, and hurries to ROXANE.)

DE GUICHE
(To ROXANE)
Well, what have you decided?

ROXANE
I'm staying!

DE GUICHE
You must leave!

ROXANE
No!

DE GUICHE
In that case, I'll need a musket.

CARBON
What do you mean?

DE GUICHE
I'm staying too.

CYRANO
Sir, you've finally shown pure courage!

FIRST CADET
Are you really a Gascon, in spite of your lace?

ROXANE
What! . . .

DE GUICHE
I won't leave a woman in danger.

SECOND CADET
(To the first)
I think we can give him something to eat!
(The food reappears as though by magic.)

DE GUICHE
(His face lighting up)
Food!

THIRD CADET
It's coming out from under every cloak!

DE GUICHE
(Haughtily, controlling himself)
Do you think I'm going to eat your leavings?

CYRANO
(Bowing)
You're making progress!

DE GUICHE
(Proudly)
An empty belly won't stop me from fighting!

FIRST CADET
(Enthusiastically)
Spoken like a Gascon!

DE GUICHE
(Laughing)
I *am* a Gascon!

FIRST CADET
It's true! He's really one of us!
(They all begin to dance.)

CARBON
(Reappearing on the parapet, after having disappeared behind the embankment a few moments earlier)
I've stationed my pikemen. They're ready to fight to the end!
(Points to a row of pikes showing above the parapet.)

DE GUICHE
(To ROXANE, bowing)
Will you accept my hand and go with me to inspect them?
(She takes his hand and they go upstage toward the

embankment. The others follow them, taking off their hats.)

CHRISTIAN
(Hurrying to CYRANO*)*
Tell me what you have to say, quickly!
(As ROXANE *appears on the parapet, the pikes disappear, lowered in a salute, and a shout arises. She bows.)*

THE PIKEMEN
(Offstage)
Hurrah!

CHRISTIAN
What's your secret?

CYRANO
If Roxane should . . .

CHRISTIAN
Yes?

CYRANO
If she should speak to you about the letters . . .

CHRISTIAN
Go on!

CYRANO
Don't make the mistake of being surprised if . . .

CHRISTIAN
If what?

CYRANO
I must tell you! . . . It's quite simple. I thought of it as soon as she arrived. You've . . .

CHRISTIAN
Tell me quickly!

CYRANO
You've . . . you've written to her more often than you think.

CHRISTIAN
I have?

CYRANO

Yes. I made myself the interpreter of your passion. I sometimes wrote to her without telling you so.

CHRISTIAN

Oh?

CYRANO

It's quite simple!

CHRISTIAN

But we're blockaded! How did you send those letters?

CYRANO

I was able to get through the enemy lines before dawn.

CHRISTIAN
   (Folding his arms)
And I suppose that was quite simple too? . . . How often have I been writing? Twice a week? Three times? Four?

CYRANO

More than that.

CHRISTIAN

Every day?

CYRANO

Yes, every day . . . twice.

CHRISTIAN
   (Violently)
And you were carried away by the letters you wrote! So much so that you defied death . . .

CYRANO
   (Seeing ROXANE *returning)*
Quiet! Not in front of her!
   (He quickly goes into his tent.)

Scene VIII

Roxane, Christian; in the background, Cadets coming and going, with Carbon and De Guiche giving orders.

ROXANE

(Hurrying to CHRISTIAN*)*
And now, Christian! . . .

CHRISTIAN

(Taking her hands)
And now, Roxane, tell me why you traveled such appalling roads, infested with lawless soldiers, in order to join me here.

ROXANE

Because of your letters!

CHRISTIAN

What?

ROXANE

It's your fault if I'm in danger: your letters made me lose my reason! You've written so many of them in the last month, each more beautiful than the one before!

CHRISTIAN

Do you mean to say that because of a few love letters . . .

ROXANE

Yes! You can't know. . . . I've adored you since the evening when, under my window, you began to reveal your soul to me in a voice I'd never heard you use before, and when I read your letters it was like hearing that same voice. I could feel its tenderness enveloping me! Finally I had to come to you, no matter what the danger! Penelope wouldn't have calmly stayed home with her weaving if Ulysses had written to her as you've written to me! She would have become as ardent as Helen of Troy, thrown her work aside, and gone off to join him!

CHRISTIAN

But . . .

ROXANE

I read your letters over and over, until I began to feel faint! I knew I belonged to you totally! Each page was like a petal fallen from your soul. In every word I felt the flame of a powerful, sincere love. . . .

CHRISTIAN

Powerful and sincere? Did you really feel that in my letters, Roxane?

ROXANE

Oh, yes!

CHRISTIAN

And so you came. . . .

ROXANE

I had to. I'm yours, Christian, but I know you would lift me up if I tried to kneel before you, so I'm placing my soul at your feet, and it will always remain there! I've come to ask you to forgive me—and now is the time to ask forgiveness, since we may be about to die!—for having insulted you, in my frivolity, by first loving you only because you were handsome.

CHRISTIAN

(In consternation)
Oh, Roxane!

ROXANE

Later, when I became a little less frivolous, I was like a bird hopping before taking flight, held back by your handsome face and drawn forward by your soul. I then loved you for both of them together.

CHRISTIAN

And now?

ROXANE

Your true self has prevailed over your outer appearance. I now love you for your soul alone.

CHRISTIAN

(Stepping back)
Oh, Roxane!

ROXANE

I know how painful it is for a noble heart to be loved because of an accident of nature that will soon pass away. But you can be happy now: your thoughts out-shine your face. Your handsomeness was what first attracted me, but now that my eyes are open I no longer see it!

CHRISTIAN

Oh! . . .

ROXANE

Do you still doubt your victory?

CHRISTIAN

(Sorrowfully)
Roxane . . .

ROXANE

I understand. You can't believe in that kind of love.

CHRISTIAN

I don't want it! I want to be loved simply for . . .

ROXANE

For what women have always loved in you till now? Let me love you in a better way!

CHRISTIAN

No! It was better before!

ROXANE

You don't know what you're saying! It's better now! I didn't really love you before. It's what makes you yourself that I now love. If you were less handsome . . .

CHRISTIAN

Enough!

ROXANE

I'd still love you. If you suddenly became ugly . . .

CHRISTIAN

Oh, don't say that!

ROXANE

I *will* say it!

CHRISTIAN

Even if I were ugly? . . .

ROXANE

Yes, even if you were ugly! I swear I'd still love you!

CHRISTIAN

My God!

ROXANE

Now are you happy?

CHRISTIAN
(Choking)
Yes. . . .

ROXANE

What's the matter?

CHRISTIAN
(Gently pushing her away)
Nothing. I must go and say a few words to someone. It will take only a minute.

ROXANE

But . . .

CHRISTIAN
(Pointing to a group of CADETS *in the background)*
My love has taken you away from those poor men. Go and smile at them a little, since they're about to die.

ROXANE
(Deeply moved)
Dear Christian! . . .
(She goes to the CADETS, *who eagerly but respectfully crowd around her.)*

Scene IX

Christian, Cyrano; Roxane in the background, talking with Carbon and some of the Cadets.

CHRISTIAN
(Calling outside CYRANO's *tent)*
Cyrano?

CYRANO
(Coming out of the tent, armed for battle)
Yes? Oh! How pale you are!

CHRISTIAN

She doesn't love me anymore!

CYRANO

What!

CHRISTIAN

It's you she loves!

CYRANO

No!

CHRISTIAN

She loves only my soul now!

CYRANO

No!

CHRISTIAN

Yes! That means it's you she loves—and you love her too!

CYRANO

I?

CHRISTIAN

I know it's true.

CYRANO

Yes, it's true.

CHRISTIAN

You love her with all your heart.

CYRANO

More than that.

CHRISTIAN

Tell her so!

CYRANO

No!

CHRISTIAN

Why not?

CYRANO

Look at my face!

CHRISTIAN

She would still love me if I were ugly!

CYRANO

She told you that?

CHRISTIAN

Yes!

CYRANO

I'm glad she said it, but don't believe such nonsense! Yes, I'm very glad she had that thought. . . . But don't take her at her word! Don't become ugly—she would never forgive me!

CHRISTIAN

We'll see!

CYRANO

No, no!

CHRISTIAN

Let her choose! I want you to tell her everything!

CYRANO

No! I couldn't bear that torture!

CHRISTIAN

Do you expect me to kill your happiness because I'm handsome? That would be too unjust!

CYRANO

And do you expect me to kill yours because I happen to have been born with a gift for expressing . . . what you may feel?

CHRISTIAN

Tell her everything!

CYRANO

It's cruel of you to persist in tempting me!

CHRISTIAN

I'm tired of being my own rival!

CYRANO

Christian!

CHRISTIAN

Our wedding took place in secret, without witnesses. The marriage can be broken—if we survive!

CYRANO

You still persist! . . .

CHRISTIAN

I want to be loved for myself or not at all! We'll see
what she decides. I'm going to walk to the end of the
camp, then come back. Talk to her while I'm gone, and
tell her she must choose one of us.

CYRANO

It will be you!

CHRISTIAN

I hope so! *(Calls.)* Roxane!

CYRANO

No! No!

ROXANE

(Hurrying toward them)
Yes?

CHRISTIAN

Cyrano has something important to tell you.
(She expectantly turns to CYRANO. CHRISTIAN *leaves.)*

Scene X

*Roxane, Cyrano; then Le Bret, Carbon, the Cadets, Ra-
gueneau, De Guiche, etc.*

ROXANE

Something important?

CYRANO

(Frantically)
He's leaving! . . . *(To* ROXANE*)* No, it's really
nothing. . . . You must know how he is: he often sees
importance where none exists!

ROXANE

(Anxiously)
Does he doubt what I told him? Yes, he does! I could
see he doubted it!

CYRANO
(Taking her hand)
But was it really the truth?

ROXANE
Yes, I'd love him even if he were . . .
  (Hesitates.)

CYRANO
(Smiling sadly)
The word embarrasses you in front of me?

ROXANE
No, I . . .

CYRANO
It won't hurt me! You'd love him even if he were ugly?

ROXANE
Yes! *(Several musket shots are heard offstage.)* The
shooting seems to have begun.

CYRANO
(Ardently)
Even if he were hideous?

ROXANE
Yes!

CYRANO
Disfigured?

ROXANE
Yes!

CYRANO
Grotesque?

ROXANE
Nothing could make him seem grotesque to me!

CYRANO
You'd still love him?

ROXANE
Yes! Maybe even more!

CYRANO
(Aside, losing his head)
My God! Perhaps it's true! Can it be that happiness is
here, within my grasp? *(To* ROXANE*)* I . . . Roxane . . .
Listen to me. . . .

LE BRET
(Entering rapidly and calling softly)
Cyrano!

CYRANO
(Turning around)
Yes?

LE BRET
Sh!
(Whispers something to CYRANO, *who lets go of* ROX-
ANE*'s hand with a cry.)*

CYRANO
Oh!

ROXANE
What's the matter?

CYRANO
(To himself, dazed)
It's all over now.
(More shots are heard.)

ROXANE
What is it? Those shots . . .
(Takes a few steps and looks offstage.)

CYRANO
It's all over. Now I can never tell her!

ROXANE
What's happened?

CYRANO
(Stopping her as she is about to rush forward)
Nothing!
(Some CADETS *have entered, hiding the burden they
are carrying. They group themselves to prevent* ROX-
ANE *from approaching.)*

ROXANE
Those men . . .

CYRANO

(Leading her away)
Come away from them!

ROXANE

But what were you about to tell me?

CYRANO

Tell you? Oh, nothing. . . . Nothing, I swear! *(Solemnly)*
I swear that Christian's mind and soul were . . . *(Catches
himself in alarm.)* . . . are the greatest . . .

ROXANE

Were?
(She screams, runs to the group of CADETS, *and
pushes them aside.)*

CYRANO

It's all over.

ROXANE

(Seeing CHRISTIAN *lying wrapped in his cloak)*
Christian!

LE BRET

(To CYRANO)
The first shot fired by the enemy!
(ROXANE throws herself onto CHRISTIAN. *More shots.
Clatter of weapons. Voices. Drumbeats.)*

CARBON

(Holding his drawn sword)
Here comes the attack! Get ready!
(Followed by the CADETS, *he climbs over the
parapet.)*

ROXANE

Christian!

CARBON'S VOICE

(From the other side of the embankment)
Hurry!

ROXANE

Christian!

CARBON

Fall in!

ROXANE

Christian!

CARBON

Prepare your matches!*
(RAGUENEAU hurries onstage, bringing water in a helmet.)

CHRISTIAN

(In a dying voice)
Roxane . . .

CYRANO

(Speaking rapidly and softly in CHRISTIAN's ear while ROXANE, distraught, tears a strip of cloth from her dress and dips it in the water to wash his wound)
I told her everything. It's still you she loves!
(CHRISTIAN closes his eyes.)

ROXANE

Yes, my love?

CARBON

Take out your ramrods!

ROXANE

(To CYRANO)
He's not dead, is he?

CARBON

Bite open your charges!

ROXANE

I feel his cheek turning cold against mine!

CARBON

Ready! Aim!

ROXANE

Here's a letter he was carrying! *(Opens it.)* For me!

---

* The match was the piece of burning cord used to set off the powder charge of a matchlock musket.

CYRANO

(Aside)
My letter!

CARBON

Fire!
(Shots. Cries. Sounds of battle.)

CYRANO

(Trying to draw his hand away from ROXANE, *who clutches it, kneeling)*
Roxane! The attack has begun!

ROXANE

(Holding him back)
Stay a little longer. He's dead. You were the only one who knew him. *(She weeps gently.)* He was a great and wonderful man, wasn't he?

CYRANO

(Standing, bareheaded)
Yes, Roxane.

ROXANE

A brilliant, captivating poet!

CYRANO

Yes, Roxane.

ROXANE

A magnificent mind!

CYRANO

Yes, Roxane.

ROXANE

A vast heart whose depths remained hidden from the world! A noble and charming soul!

CYRANO

(Firmly)
Yes, Roxane!

ROXANE

(Throwing herself onto CHRISTIAN'*s body)*
He's dead!

CYRANO

(Aside, drawing his sword)
And now I too must die, since, without knowing it, she's
mourning for me in him!
*(Trumpets in the distance. DE GUICHE reappears on
the parapet, bareheaded, with a wound on his forehead.)*

DE GUICHE

(In a thunderous voice)
That's the signal! A fanfare! The French are on their
way back to camp with provisions! Hold fast a little
longer!

ROXANE

There's blood on his letter, and tears!

A VOICE

(Shouting from the other side of the embankment)
Surrender!

CADETS' VOICES

No!

RAGUENEAU

*(Who has climbed up on his carriage to watch the
battle beyond the embankment)*
They're coming closer!

CYRANO

(To DE GUICHE, pointing to ROXANE)
Take her away! I'm going to charge!

ROXANE

(Feebly, kissing the letter)
His blood! His tears!

RAGUENEAU

*(Leaping down from the carriage and running toward
her)*
She's fainted!

DE GUICHE

(On the parapet, shouting fiercely to the CADETS)
Hold fast!

A VOICE
(From beyond the embankment)
Lay down your arms!

CADETS' VOICES
No!

CYRANO
(To DE GUICHE*)*
You've proved your valor, sir. *(Points to* ROXANE.*)* Flee now, and save her!

DE GUICHE
(Hurrying to ROXANE *and picking her up in his arms)*
I'll do it, for her sake. But we can win if you gain time!

CYRANO
We will! *(Watches* ROXANE, *unconscious, being carried away by* DE GUICHE *and* RAGUENEAU.*)* Good-by, Roxane!
(Tumult. Shouts. CADETS *reappear, wounded, and fall onstage.* CYRANO, *rushing toward the battle, is stopped on the parapet by* CARBON, *covered with blood.)*

CARBON
We're giving ground! I've been wounded twice!

CYRANO
(Shouting to the CADETS *in their native Gascon tongue)*
Hardi! Reculès pas, drollos! *(To* CARBON, *holding him up)* Don't give up hope! I have two deaths to avenge: Christian's and that of my happiness! *(They go downstage.* CYRANO *brandishes the lance to which* ROXANE's *handkerchief is tied.)* Float proudly, little lace banner bearing her monogram! *(Plants it on the parapet and again shouts to the* CADETS.*)* Toumbé dèssus! Escrasas lous! *(To the fifer)* Play your fife!
(The fifer plays. Some of the wounded men stand up. Other CADETS *come down the embankment and group themselves around* CYRANO *and the little flag. The carriage is filled and covered with men. Bristling with muskets, it is transformed into a redoubt. A*

CADET *appears on the parapet, moving backward, still fighting.)*

THE CADET
(Shouting)
They're coming up the embankment!
(He falls dead.)

CYRANO
We'll give them a salute!
(In an instant the parapet is crowned by a formidable line of enemy soldiers. Large Imperial banners are raised.)

CYRANO
Fire!
(General volley)

A VOICE
(Shouting from the enemy ranks)
Fire!
(Murderous counterfire. CADETS fall on all sides.)

A SPANISH OFFICER
Who are these men who have such scorn for death?

CYRANO
(Reciting, facing the enemy fire)
These are the stouthearted Gascon Cadets
Of Carbon de Castel-Jaloux;
They fight over trifles and shamelessly lie. . . .
(He rushes forward, followed by the few survivors.)
These are the stouthearted Gascon . . .
(The rest is lost in the tumult of battle.)

CURTAIN

Act Five

❦

Cyrano's Gazette

Fifteen years later, in 1655. The park of the convent occupied by the Ladies of the Cross, in Paris.

Magnificent, shady foliage. To the left, the house, whose front steps lead up to a broad landing with several doors opening onto it. An enormous tree in the middle of the stage, standing alone in a small oval-shaped open space. Downstage right, a semicircular stone bench among large box shrubs.

A lane bordered by chestnut trees crosses the entire background and ends at the door of a chapel on the right, half hidden among the branches. Beyond the lane, seen through the double row of chestnut trees, are stretches of lawn, other lanes, groves, the depths of the park, and the sky.

A side door of the chapel opens into a colonnade, entwined by reddened vines, which vanishes behind the box shrubs downstage right.

It is autumn. The foliage above the green lawn has turned red. Spots of darker color formed by box shrubs and yew trees that have remained green. A carpet of yellow leaves under each tree. Dead leaves are strewn over the whole stage; they crackle underfoot along the lanes, and half cover the bench and the landing at the top of the front steps.

Between the bench on the right and the tree, a large

*embroidery frame with a small chair in front of it.
Baskets full of skeins and balls of thread. A tapestry
has been begun in the frame.*

As the curtain rises, NUNS *are coming and going
in the park. Some are seated on the bench, around
an older* NUN. *Leaves are falling.*

Scene I

*Mother Marguerite, Sister Marthe, Sister Claire, other
Nuns.*

SISTER MARTHE
(To MOTHER MARGUERITE*)*
Sister Claire has stopped in front of the mirror twice, to
see how her headdress looks.

MOTHER MARGUERITE
(To SISTER CLAIRE*)*
That's odious.

SISTER CLAIRE
But Sister Marthe took a prune from the tart this morning. I saw her!

MOTHER MARGUERITE
(To SISTER MARTHE*)*
That's disgraceful, Sister Marthe.

SISTER CLAIRE
One little look!

SISTER MARTHE
One little prune!

MOTHER MARGUERITE
(Sternly)
I'll tell Monsieur Cyrano this evening.

SISTER CLAIRE
(Alarmed)
No! He'll make fun of us!

SISTER MARTHE
He'll say that nuns are very coquettish!

SISTER CLAIRE
And very greedy!

MOTHER MARGUERITE
(Smiling)
And very good.

SISTER CLAIRE
He's been coming every Saturday for the past ten years, hasn't he, Mother Marguerite de Jésus?

MOTHER MARGUERITE
Longer than that! Ever since his cousin came to us fourteen years ago, mingling her black mourning veil with our linen hoods, like a raven among a flock of white doves.

SISTER MARTHE
In all the time since she first took a room in this cloister, no one but Monsieur Cyrano has ever been able to distract her from the grief that afflicts her night and day.

ALL THE NUNS
He's so amusing!—His visits are delightful!—He teases us!—Such a nice man!—We all like him!—He always appreciates the pastry we make for him!

SISTER MARTHE
But he's not a very good Catholic!

SISTER CLAIRE
We'll convert him.

OTHER NUNS
Yes! Yes!

MOTHER MARGUERITE
I forbid you to make any efforts in that direction, my children. Don't torment him: he might come less often!

SISTER MARTHE
But God . . .

MOTHER MARGUERITE
Have no fear: I'm sure God knows him well.

SISTER MARTHE

But when he comes in every Saturday he says to me
proudly, "Sister, I ate meat yesterday!"

MOTHER MARGUERITE

Oh? Is that what he tells you? Well, the last time he
came, he hadn't eaten anything for two days.

SISTER MARTHE

Oh, Mother!

MOTHER MARGUERITE

He's poor.

SISTER MARTHE

Who told you so?

MOTHER MARGUERITE

Monsieur Le Bret.

SISTER MARTHE

Doesn't anyone help him?

MOTHER MARGUERITE

No. It would only make him angry if anyone tried. (ROX-
ANE *appears, walking slowly along a lane in the background. She is dressed in black, with a widow's cap and
long veils.* DE GUICHE, *who has aged gracefully, walks
beside her.* MOTHER MARGUERITE *stands up.*) Come, we
must go inside. Madame Magdeleine is strolling in the
park with a visitor.

SISTER MARTHE

(Softly, to SISTER CLAIRE*)*
It's the Marshal Duke de Grammont, isn't it?

SISTER CLAIRE

(Looking)
Yes, I think so.

SISTER MARTHE

This is the first time he's come to see her for months!

OTHER NUNS

He's very busy.—The court.—The army. . . .

SISTER CLAIRE

Worldly concerns!

(The NUNS *leave.* DE GUICHE *and* ROXANE *come downstage in silence and stop near the embroidery frame. Several moments pass.)*

Scene II

Roxane, the Duke de Grammont (formerly Count de Guiche), then Le Bret and Ragueneau.

THE DUKE

And so you remain here, letting your blond beauty go to waste, still in mourning?

ROXANE

Still in mourning.

THE DUKE

And still faithful?

ROXANE

Still faithful.

THE DUKE
    (After a moment of silence)
Have you forgiven me?

ROXANE
    (Simply, looking at the cross of the convent)
Of course, since I'm here.
    (Another silence.)

THE DUKE

Was he really such a . . .

ROXANE

He showed his true nature only to those who knew him well.

THE DUKE

His true nature? . . . Yes, perhaps I didn't know him well enough. . . . Do you still carry his last letter over your heart?

ROXANE

Yes, like a holy relic.

THE DUKE

You love him even in death?

ROXANE

Sometimes it seems to me that he's not really dead. I feel that our hearts are together, and that his love floats around me, very much alive!

THE DUKE

(After another silence)
Does Cyrano come to see you?

ROXANE

Yes, often. My old friend gives me all the news; he replaces the gazettes for me. He visits me regularly. If the weather is good, his chair is always brought out and placed under this tree. I embroider while I wait for him. When the clock strikes the hour of his arrival, I don't even turn around to look for him, because I know I'll hear his cane coming down the steps immediately after the last stroke. He sits down and laughs at my eternal tapestry. Then he begins telling me about the week's happenings, and . . . *(LE BRET appears on the steps.)* Ah! Here's Le Bret! *(LE BRET comes down.)* How is our friend doing?

LE BRET

Badly.

THE DUKE

Oh!

ROXANE

(To the DUKE)
He's exaggerating!

LE BRET

Cyrano is living in isolation and poverty, just as I predicted! His writings constantly make new enemies for him! He attacks false noblemen, false saints, false heroes, plagiarists—everyone!

ROXANE

But his sword fills everyone with terror. No one will ever get the best of him.

THE DUKE

(Shaking his head)
Who knows?

LE BRET

I'm not afraid of his meeting a violent death. Loneliness,
hunger, the cold of winter creeping into his dark room—
those are the assassins that will end his life! He tightens
his belt one more notch every day, his poor nose has
turned as pale as ivory, he has only one threadbare
black coat. . . .

THE DUKE

It's certainly true that he hasn't scaled the heights of
worldly success, but don't feel too sorry for him.

LE BRET

(With a bitter smile)
Sir, you . . .

THE DUKE

No, don't feel too sorry for him: he lives without compromise, free in both his thoughts and his acts.

LE BRET

(Still smiling bitterly)
Sir, you . . .

THE DUKE

(Loftily)
Yes, I know: I have everything and he has nothing. But
I'd be honored to shake his hand. *(Bows to* ROXANE.*)* I
must go. Good-by.

ROXANE

I'll accompany you to the door.
(The DUKE *bows to* LE BRET *and walks toward the
steps with* ROXANE.*)*

THE DUKE

(Stopping as they are climbing the steps)
Yes, sometimes I envy him. When a man has been too
successful in life, even though he hasn't done anything
really wrong, he still has all sorts of reasons for feeling
a little disgusted with himself. Their combined weight
isn't enough to form a burden of remorse, but he can

never escape a kind of vague uneasiness. As he continues to climb toward even greater success, he hears dead illusions and old regrets rustling under his ducal mantle, like the fallen leaves swept along by the train of your black dress when you mount these steps.

ROXANE
(Ironically)
You're in a thoughtful mood today.

THE DUKE
Yes, I'm afraid so. *(Abruptly, just as he is about to leave)* Monsieur Le Bret! *(To ROXANE)* Will you excuse me? I want to have a word with him. *(Goes to LE BRET and speaks in a low voice.)* It's true that no one would dare to attack our friend openly, but it's also true that he's hated by many people. Only yesterday, during a card game at court, someone said to me, "That Cyrano may have a fatal accident someday."

LE BRET
Oh?

THE DUKE
Yes. Tell him not to go out very often, and to be careful.

LE BRET
(Throwing up his arms)
Careful! . . . He'll soon be here; I'll warn him. But . . .

ROXANE
(Who has remained on the steps, to a NUN coming toward her)
What is it?

THE NUN
Ragueneau would like to see you, madame.

ROXANE
Bring him in. *(To the DUKE and LE BRET)* He's come to complain about his poverty. Since the day when he set out to be a writer, he's been a singer . . .

LE BRET
A bathhouse attendant . . .

ROXANE

An actor . . .

LE BRET

A beadle . . .

ROXANE

A hairdresser . . .

LE BRET

A lute teacher . . .

ROXANE

What can he have become now?

RAGUENEAU
(Entering rapidly)
Ah, madame! *(Sees* LE BRET.*)* Sir!

ROXANE
(Smiling)
Tell Le Bret your troubles. I'll be back soon.

RAGUENEAU

But madame . . .
*(*ROXANE *ignores him and leaves with the* DUKE. RA-GUENEAU *goes to* LE BRET.*)*

Scene III

Le Bret, Ragueneau.

RAGUENEAU
Since you're here, I'd rather she didn't know. . . . As I was approaching our friend's house this afternoon, on my way to visit him, I saw him come out. I hurried to catch up with him. I can't say for certain that it wasn't an accident, but when he was about to turn the corner a lackey dropped a piece of firewood on him from an upstairs window.

LE BRET
The cowards! . . . Cyrano! . . .

RAGUENEAU

I ran to him. . . .

LE BRET

It's horrible!

RAGUENEAU

Our friend, sir, our poet, was lying on the ground with a big hole in his head!

LE BRET

Is he dead?

RAGUENEAU

No, but . . . My God! . . . I carried him back into his house, to his room, rather. Oh, that room! What a wretched little closet!

LE BRET

Is he in pain?

RAGUENEAU

No, sir, he's unconscious.

LE BRET

Did you bring a doctor?

RAGUENEAU

Yes, I found one who was willing to come out of charity.

LE BRET

Poor Cyrano! . . . We mustn't tell Roxane all at once. . . . What did the doctor say?

RAGUENEAU

I don't remember very clearly, something about fever, and the meninges. . . . Oh, if you'd seen him lying there, with his head wrapped in bandages! . . . Come with me quickly! There's no one with him now, and he may die if he tries to get up!

LE BRET

(Leading him to the right)
Let's go this way, through the chapel. It's shorter.
(ROXANE appears on the steps and sees LE BRET hur-rying along the colonnade that leads to the side door of the chapel.)

ROXANE

Monsieur Le Bret! *(LE BRET and RAGUENEAU leave without answering.)* Le Bret runs away when I call him? Poor Ragueneau must really be in trouble this time!
(She comes down the steps.)

Scene IV

Roxane, alone; then two Nuns, briefly.

ROXANE

What a beautiful autumn day! Even my sorrow is smiling. It's offended by April, but gives in to the gentler charm of September. *(She sits down in front of her embroidery frame. Two NUNS come out of the house, carrying a large armchair, and set it down under a tree.)* Ah, here's the chair for my old friend!

SISTER MARTHE

It's the best one in the visiting room!

ROXANE

Thank you, Sister. *(The NUNS leave.)* He'll soon be here. *(She begins working. The clock strikes.)* There, it's time. I'll take out my skeins. . . . This is surprising: the clock has finished striking and he's not here yet. Is he going to be late for the first time? The Sister at the door must be—Where's my thimble? There, I see it—must be trying to persuade him to repent of his sins. *(Several moments pass.)* Still persuading him! He'll surely be here before long. . . . A dead leaf. . . . *(She brushes aside the leaf that has fallen onto the embroidery frame.)* Nothing could—My scissors . . . in my bag!—prevent him from coming!

A NUN

(Appearing on the steps)
Monsieur de Bergerac is here.

Scene V

Roxane, Cyrano, and briefly, Sister Marthe.

ROXANE
(Without turning around)
I knew it! *(She continues her work.* CYRANO *appears. He is very pale, and his hat is pulled down over his eyes. The* NUN *who has accompanied him leaves. He slowly comes down the steps, leaning on his cane and making an obvious effort to stay on his feet.* ROXANE *is still working.)* Oh, these faded colors! . . . How will I ever match them? *(To* CYRANO, *in a tone of friendly rebuke)* Late, for the first time in fourteen years!

(CYRANO has succeeded in reaching his chair and sitting down in it. When he speaks, his cheerful voice contrasts with his face.)

CYRANO
Yes, it's scandalous! I can't tell you how annoyed I am. I was delayed by . . .

ROXANE
By what?

CYRANO
By an untimely visit.

ROXANE
(Distractedly, still working)
A friend of yours?

CYRANO
An old acquaintance. We've met on the battlefield, among other places. I knew we'd meet again some day, but this wasn't the time for it.

ROXANE
You sent him away?

CYRANO
Yes, I said to him, "Excuse me, but this is Saturday, the day when I always keep a certain appointment. Nothing can make me miss it. Come back in an hour."

ROXANE

(Lightly)
Well, I'm afraid he'll have to wait for you, because I won't let you leave before nightfall.

CYRANO

(Gently)
I may have to leave a little sooner than that.
(He closes his eyes and remains silent. SISTER MARTHE *walks across the park, from the chapel to the steps.* ROXANE *sees her and nods to her.)*

ROXANE

(To CYRANO*)*
Aren't you going to tease Sister Marthe today?

CYRANO

(Quickly, opening his eyes)
Yes, of course! *(In a comically gruff voice)* Sister Marthe! Come here! *(She comes to him.)* When you have such lovely eyes, why do you keep them cast down?

SISTER MARTHE

(Looking up with a smile)
I . . . *(Sees his face and makes a gesture of astonishment.)* Oh!

CYRANO

(In an undertone, pointing to ROXANE*)*
Sh! It's nothing. . . . *(Loudly and truculently)* I ate meat yesterday!

SISTER MARTHE

I know. *(Aside)* He's pale from hunger! *(Rapidly, in a low voice)* Come to the dining hall in a little while and I'll give you a big bowl of soup. Will you come?

CYRANO

Yes, yes, yes.

SISTER MARTHE

Ah, you're a little more sensible today!

ROXANE

(Who has heard them whispering)
She's trying to convert you!

SISTER MARTHE

I'm doing no such thing!

CYRANO

Now that I think of it, you're always full of pious plati-
tudes, yet you never preach to me! It's amazing! *(With
mock ferocity)* I'll show you that you're not the only one
who can be amazing! Just listen to this! I'm going to . . .
(Seems to be trying to think of a good way to tease her.)
Ah! I've got it! I'm going to allow you to pray for me
tonight in the chapel!

ROXANE

Oh! Oh!

CYRANO

(Laughing)
Sister Marthe is dumbfounded!

SISTER MARTHE

(Gently)
I haven't waited for your permission.
(She goes into the house.)

CYRANO

(Turning back to ROXANE, *who is leaning over her
work)*
May the devil take me if I ever see that tapestry finished!

ROXANE

I was expecting some such remark.
(A breeze makes some leaves fall.)

CYRANO

The leaves . . .

ROXANE

(Raising her head and looking into the distance)
They're Titian red. . . . Look at them falling.

CYRANO

How well they fall! Such beauty in that short drop from
branch to earth! Despite their terror of rotting on the
ground, they give their fall the grace of flight.

ROXANE

Can it be that you're melancholy—you?

CYRANO
(Catching himself)
Not at all!

ROXANE
Then forget about the falling leaves and tell me the latest news. Aren't you still my gazette?

CYRANO
I'll begin this very moment.

ROXANE
Good.

CYRANO
(More and more pale, struggling against his pain)
Last Saturday, the nineteenth, after eating eight helpings of preserved fruit, the King took to his bed with a fever; his illness was convicted of high treason and executed by his physician, and since then the royal pulse has returned to normal. At the Queen's ball on Sunday, seven hundred and sixty-three white wax candles were burned. Our troops are reported to have beaten John of Austria.* Four sorcerers have been hanged. Madame d'Athis's little dog had to be given an enema to . . .

ROXANE
That will do, Monsieur de Bergerac!

CYRANO
On Monday . . . nothing. Lygdamire took a new lover.

ROXANE
Oh!

CYRANO
(Whose face is increasingly twisted by pain)
On Tuesday, the whole court went to Fontainebleau. On Wednesday, Madame Montglat said no to Count de Fiesque. On Thursday, Olympe Mancini† was the Queen of France—or almost! On Friday, the twenty-fifth, Ma-

---

* John of Austria (1629–79), Spanish general defeated by the French in Flanders.

† Olympe Mancini (1639–1708), one of Louis XIV's mistresses, who briefly had hopes of marrying him.

dame Montglat said yes to Count de Fiesque. And today, Saturday the twenty-sixth . . .

(He closes his eyes and his head falls. Silence. Surprised at no longer hearing him speak, ROXANE *turns and looks at him, then stands up in alarm.)*

ROXANE

Has he fainted? *(Hurries to him with a cry.)* Cyrano!

CYRANO

(Vaguely, opening his eyes)
What is it? . . . What . . . *(Seeing her leaning over him, he quickly puts his hand to his hat to make sure it is still pulled down, and draws away from her in his chair.)* No! It's nothing, believe me! Go back to your chair.

ROXANE

But you . . .

CYRANO

It's only my old wound from Arras. Sometimes it . . . You know. . . .

ROXANE

My poor friend!

CYRANO

It's really nothing. It will soon go away. *(Smiles with an effort.)* There, it's gone.

ROXANE

(Standing beside him)
Each of us has his wound. Mine is old but still unhealed, here . . . *(Puts her hand to her bosom.)* . . . under the yellowed paper of a letter still stained with tears and blood!

(Twilight is beginning to fall.)

CYRANO

His letter! . . . Didn't you once tell me that you might let me read it some day?

ROXANE

You want to read . . . his letter?

CYRANO

Yes, I do. Now.

ROXANE

(Removing the little bag that hangs from around her neck)

Here!

CYRANO

(Taking it)

May I open it?

ROXANE

Yes, read it.

(She goes back to the embroidery frame and begins putting away her thread.)

CYRANO

(Reading)

"Farewell, Roxane! Death is near. . . ."

ROXANE

(Stopping in surprise)

You're reading it aloud?

CYRANO

(Reading)

"I believe this will be my last day, my beloved. My soul is still heavy with unexpressed love, and I must die! Never again will my eyes delight . . ."

ROXANE

How well you read his letter!

CYRANO

(Continuing)

". . . will my eyes delight in kissing each of your graceful gestures. I remember one of them, a way of putting your hand to your forehead, and I want to cry out . . ."

ROXANE

(Troubled)

How well you read . . . that letter!

(The twilight is turning to darkness.)

CYRANO

". . . to cry out, 'Good-by!' . . ."

ROXANE

You read it . . .

CYRANO

". . . my dearest, my darling, my treasure . . ."

ROXANE

(Thoughtfully)
. . . in a voice that . . .

CYRANO

". . . my love!"

ROXANE

. . . that . . . *(She starts.)* A voice that I'm not hearing
for the first time!
*(She slowly approaches him without his seeing her,
stands behind his chair, silently bends down, and
looks at the letter. The darkness is deepening.)*

CYRANO

"My heart has never left you for a moment, and in the
next world my love for you will still be as boundless,
as . . ."

ROXANE

(Putting her hand on his shoulder)
How can you read now? It's dark. *(He starts, turns
around, sees her standing close to him, makes a gesture
of alarm, and bows his head. A long silence. Then, in the
shadowy darkness, she clasps her hands and speaks
slowly.)* And for fourteen years you played the part of
an old friend who came to be amusing!

CYRANO

Roxane!

ROXANE

It was you.

CYRANO

No, Roxane, no!

ROXANE

I should have guessed it each time I heard you say my
name!

CYRANO

No! It wasn't . . .

ROXANE

It *was* you!

CYRANO

I swear . . .

ROXANE

I see the whole selfless imposture now! The letters . . .
It was you.

CYRANO

No!

ROXANE

The wild, endearing words . . . It was you.

CYRANO

No!

ROXANE

The voice in the night . . . It was you.

CYRANO

I swear it wasn't!

ROXANE

The soul . . . It was yours!

CYRANO

I didn't love you!

ROXANE

You did love me!

CYRANO

(Desperately)
It was Christian!

ROXANE

You loved me!

CYRANO
(In a weakening voice)
No!

ROXANE

You already deny it less strongly!

CYRANO

No, no, my love, I didn't love you!

ROXANE

Ah, how many things have died, and how many have
now been born! Why were you silent for fourteen years,
knowing that he hadn't written that letter, and that the
tears on it were yours?

CYRANO

(Handing her the letter)
The blood was his.

ROXANE

And why have you let that sublime silence be broken
this evening?

CYRANO

Why? . . .
    *(*LE BRET *and* RAGUENEAU *enter, running.)*

Scene VI

Cyrano, Roxane, Le Bret, Ragueneau.

LE BRET

What foolhardiness! I knew we'd find him here!

CYRANO

(Smiling, and sitting more erect)
You were right. Here I am.

LE BRET

(To ROXANE*)*
He's killed himself by leaving his bed!

ROXANE

Oh, God! . . . *(To* CYRANO*)* Your faintness a little while
ago . . . Was it . . .

CYRANO

That reminds me: I didn't finish my gazette! Today, Saturday the twenty-sixth, an hour before dinnertime, Monsieur de Bergerac was murdered.

(He takes off his hat, showing the bandages around his head.)

ROXANE

What is he saying? . . . Cyrano! . . . Those bandages! . . . What have they done to you? Why?

CYRANO

"To be struck down by the only noble weapon, the sword, wielded by an adversary worthy of me . . ." Yes, I once said that. Fate is a great jester! I've been struck down, but from behind, in an ambush, by a lackey wielding a log! I've been consistent to the end. I've failed in everything, even in my death.

RAGUENEAU

Oh, sir! . . .

CYRANO

Don't weep so loudly, Ragueneau. *(Takes his hand.)* Tell me, brother poet, what are you doing these days?

RAGUENEAU

(Through his tears)

I'm the candle-snuffer in a theater . . . Molière's* company. . . .

CYRANO

Molière!

RAGUENEAU

Yes, but I'm leaving him tomorrow. I'm outraged! Yesterday they played his *Scapin,* and I saw that he'd taken a scene from you!

LE BRET

A whole scene!

RAGUENEAU

Yes, sir, the famous "What the devil was he doing? . . ."

---

* Molière (1622–73, real name Jean-Baptiste Poquelin), the great French comic playwright, had his own theatrical company, for which he wrote his plays.

LE BRET

(Furious)
Molière took it from you!

CYRANO

Be calm. He was right to take it. *(To* RAGUENEAU*)* How
did the audience react to the scene?

RAGUENEAU

(Sobbing)
Oh, sir, they laughed and laughed!

CYRANO

Yes, my life has been that of a man who provides words
and ideas for others, spurs them to action, and is then
forgotten. *(To* ROXANE*)* Do you remember the evening
when Christian spoke to you below your balcony? Well,
that evening was the essence of my life: while I remained
below, in the shadows, others climbed up to receive the
kiss of glory. But now, on the threshold of my grave, I
acknowledge the justice of it all—Molière is a genius,
and Christian was handsome! *(The chapel bell has begun
ringing; the* NUNS *are now seen walking along the lane in
the background, on their way to Vespers.)* Let them go
to their prayers, since their bell is ringing.

ROXANE

(Looking up and calling)
Sister! Sister!

CYRANO

(Holding her back)
No, no, don't go to bring anyone! You'd find me gone
when you returned. *(The* NUNS *have entered the chapel,
and the organ is heard.)* I needed a little harmony, and
there it is.

ROXANE

I love you! You must live!

CYRANO

No. In the fairy tale, when Beauty said, "I love you,"
to the prince, his ugliness melted away like snow in the
warmth of the sun, but as you can see, those words have
no such magic effect on me.

ROXANE

Your life has been unhappy because of me! Me!

CYRANO

No, Roxane, quite the contrary. Feminine sweetness was
unknown to me. My mother made it clear that she didn't
find me pleasant to look at. I had no sister. Later, I
dreaded the thought of seeing mockery in the eyes of a
mistress. Thanks to you, I've at least had a woman's
friendship, a gracious presence to soften the harsh loneliness of my life.

LE BRET
   *(Pointing to the moonlight shining through the
   branches)*
Your other friend has come to visit you.

CYRANO
   (Smiling at the moon)
Yes, I see her.

ROXANE

I've loved only one man, and I've lost him twice!

CYRANO

Le Bret, I'll soon be soaring up to the moon, this time
without having to invent a machine. . . .

ROXANE

The moon?

CYRANO

Yes, of course, that's where I'll be sent to find my para-
dise. More than one soul that I love must be exiled
there. I'll be with Socrates, Galileo. . . .

LE BRET
   (Rebelling)
No! No! A man like you, a poet with such a great and
noble heart—you can't die this way! It's too stupid!
Too unjust!

CYRANO

There's Le Bret—always complaining!

LE BRET
   (Bursting into tears)
My dear friend . . .

CYRANO

(Half raising himself from his chair, with a distraught look in his eyes)

These are the stouthearted Gascon Cadets. . . . The elemental mass . . . Ah, yes . . . There's the difficulty. . . .

LE BRET

His learning stays with him, even in his delirium.

CYRANO

Copernicus said . . .

ROXANE

Oh!

CYRANO

But what the devil was he . . . what the devil was he doing there? . . . "Philosopher, scientist, poet, swordsman, musician, aerial traveler, maker of sharp retorts, and lover (not to his advantage!), here lies Savinien de Cyrano de Bergerac, who was everything, and who was nothing." Excuse me, I must go now: a moonbeam has come to take me away, and I can't keep it waiting! *(He falls back into his chair.* ROXANE's *weeping recalls him to reality. He looks at her and strokes her veils.)* I don't want you to mourn any less for that good, charming, handsome Christian; my only hope is that when the great cold has seeped into my bones, you'll give a double meaning to those black veils, and mourn for me a little when you mourn for him.

ROXANE

I swear to you that . . .

*(*CYRANO *is shaken by a great tremor, and abruptly stands up.)*

CYRANO

No! Not there! Not in a chair! *(The others move toward him.)* Stand back! I want no support from anyone! *(Leans against the tree.)* Only from this tree! *(Silence)* He's coming. I already feel stone boots . . . lead gloves. . . . *(Stiffens himself.)* Yes, he's coming, but I'll meet him on my feet . . . *(Draws his sword.)* . . . sword in hand!

LE BRET

Cyrano!

ROXANE

(Half fainting)
Cyrano!
(They all draw back in terror.)

CYRANO

I believe I see . . . yes, I see him, with his noseless face,
daring to look at my nose! *(Raises his sword.)* What's
that you say? It's useless? Of course, but I've never
needed hope of victory to make me fight! The noblest
battles are always fought in vain! . . . You there, all of
you, who are you? Your numbers seem endless. . . . Ah,
I recognize you now: my old enemies! Lies! My greetings
to you! *(Thrusts his sword into the empty air.)* And
here's Compromise! And Prejudice! And Cowardice!
(Thrusts again.) What's that? Come to terms with you?
Never! Never! . . . Ah, there you are, Stupidity! . . . I
know I can't defeat you all, I know that in the end you'll
overwhelm me, but I'll still fight you as long as there's
a breath in my body! *(Swings his sword in great arcs,
then stops, panting.)* Yes, you've robbed me of everything: the laurels of glory, the roses of love! But there's
one thing you can't take away from me. When I go to
meet God this evening, and doff my hat before the holy
gates, my salute will sweep the blue threshold of heaven,
because I'll still have one thing intact, without a stain,
something that I'll take with me in spite of you! *(Springs
forward with his sword raised.)* You ask what it is? I'll
tell you! It's . . .
*(His sword drops from his hand; he staggers and
falls into the arms of* LE BRET *and* RAGUENEAU.*)*

ROXANE

(Bending down and kissing him on the forehead)
What is it?

CYRANO

(Opening his eyes and smiling at her)
My white plume.

CURTAIN

Afterword

When the director of the Musée Grévin, the famous wax museum in Paris, asked Francis Huster how he wanted to be immortalized, the actor did not hesitate. Although he had played Hamlet, Henry IV, Don Juan, Rodrigue, Lorenzaccio, and close to a hundred other roles on the stage and screen, he instinctively chose Edmond Rostand's swashbuckling and lovesick poet, Hercule-Savinien de Cyrano de Bergerac. But why? Huster, one of the best-looking and most versatile leading men in France today, has devoted his life to theater ever since he fell in love with the tough-guy performances of John Wayne and Steve McQueen. He developed his craft at the National Conservatory of Drama with the greatest teachers of his generation. He acted for a decade at France's most prestigious national theater, the Comédie-Française, before becoming an independent actor and director and finally founding his own troupe. In À la recherche du nez perdu, his book about how he approached the role of Cyrano for Jérome Savary's groundbreaking production at the Théâtre de Chaillot, Huster emphasizes the importance of reevaluating "the hero with the long nose." He points out that playing Cyrano is the suicidal challenge in the life of an actor, since every critic, scholar, and theater lover is waiting to see what he will bring to the role. It is also, because of its very complexity and now mythical quality, an actor's dream. In the wax figure he modeled for the Grévin, Huster captured what he considered the essence of Cyrano by posing not just with the requisite cape, boots, and sword of the valiant Gascon, but also with a book and a nose, the latter held in his left hand, like a prop.

225

Long ago, another superstar, one of the most esteemed male leads in the history of theater, also posed as Cyrano for the Musée Grévin. His name was Benoît-Constant Coquelin, known in France as Coquelin aîné to differentiate him from his son, also an actor. It is Coquelin who created the title role for Edmond Rostand's masterpiece on December 28, 1897. The premiere at the Théâtre de la Porte Saint-Martin was nothing less than sensational. Cheering started in Act One, right after the Soliloquy of the Nose, only to intensify after the Ballade of the Dueling Poet. In Act Two, the rapid succession of cleverly blocked scenes and powerfully delivered speeches hit the audience like thunderbolts: the Cyrano–Roxane duo, the presentation of the Gascon Cadets, the "No, thank you" soliloquy, the tale of the One-Against-One-Hundred at the Porte de Nesle, interrupted by Christian's witticisms about Cyrano's nose. At the intermission, a cabinet minister, enthralled by what he had just witnessed, found Rostand backstage, took off his own Legion of Honor, and pinned it on the lapel of the twenty-nine-year-old playwright in anticipation of what he knew would be the actual awarding of France's most coveted distinction. It occurred, in fact, just days later.

Act Three's Balcony Scene won over the rest of the audience, skyrocketing Coquelin and Rostand to fame and fortune. Twenty-minute ovations led to forty curtain calls that kept Coquelin and his artistic team in the theater until close to daybreak. Paris had not experienced such a phenomenon since Victor Hugo's *Hernani* in 1830 and Pierre Corneille's much earlier *Le Cid* in 1637. From December 1897 to March 1899, Coquelin triumphed in more than four hundred consecutive performances, displaying night after night the multiple facets of Cyrano's outsized personality: his arrogance, passion, rage, humor, and vulnerability. One critic remarked that Coquelin made the role "thrillingly theatrical." On January 6, 1898, the president of France, Félix Faure, and his family attended the production that had theater lovers buzzing.

To understand the astounding success that was *Cyrano*, it is crucial to keep in mind the historical context of the period. In France, theatergoers had grown tired of the realism and symbolism exhibited in the latest wave of popular plays: those of Strindberg and Ibsen. Still smarting from a humiliating defeat in the Franco-Prussian War, the country was now torn apart by the Dreyfus Affair, with *Dreyfusards* and *anti-Dreyfusards* exchanging virulent public insults, base accusations of treason or anti-Semitism, and even death threats. On January 13, 1898, two weeks after the premiere of *Cyrano*, Émile Zola published his incendiary and highly controversial *"J'accuse,"* an open letter to President Faure that marked a major turning point in the history of the scandal. Thus, in the waning years of the nineteenth century, the French yearned to escape into a make-believe world of dashing young soldiers and beautiful young maidens. An idealized setting of early-seventeenth-century France provided a perfect meeting ground for those eager to forget their common shame over a lost war and their bitter divisions over a political scandal that threatened to bring down the French Republic. United in their admiration for *Cyrano*, they could applaud a riveting costume drama that was both a nostalgic return to a glorious past and a bold new theatrical experience.

By the hundredth performance, Coquelin had worn two full costumes to shreds, and Rostand wrote a letter praising him for playing the "overwhelming" role of Cyrano (*écrasant* is the French word) with such ease that he had obviously "acquired the habit of being extraordinary." "My dear friend," he added in jest, "you no longer even get tired. I feel like adding a few scenes."* By now, both Rostand and Coquelin felt confident enough to joke about such matters. They had accomplished not just a memorable feat but almost a miracle: turning a 2,560-line text in verse, a title role of 1,600 lines, five imposing sets (the spectacular Théâtre de l'Hôtel de Bourgogne, Ragueneau's Rue Saint-Honoré pastry shop, Roxane's fashionable Marais neighborhood, the battlefield at Arras, and the Ladies of the Cross convent), forty speaking roles, countless walk-ons, and hundreds of props into a three-hour-long international triumph.

* "Coquelin, Le 1er Cyrano: la 100ème représentation—photos de Nadar." *Cyrano de Bergerac: toute l'information sur Cyrano(s) de Bergerac, personnage d'Edmond de Rostand.* Web, 17 August 2011. www.cyranodebergerac.fr.

Coquelin's incomparable voice and dazzling performance quickly became legendary, capturing the hearts and minds of critics and crowds first in Paris, then in London and New York. The highly versatile and respected American character actor Richard Mansfield was so eager to understand the Cyrano phenomenon that he booked a ticket on an oceanliner and traveled to Paris to see the play for himself. For an entire week, he sat in the first row of the Théâtre de la Porte Saint-Martin, studying Coquelin's technique. He promptly bought the U.S. rights to the play, returned to New York, and staged the first American production of *Cyrano* at the Garden Theatre. The translation was signed Howard Thayer Kingsbury; opening night was October 3, 1898. Termed "a very great success" by the New York press, the show had a long, if not entirely uneventful, run. Indeed, Thomas Allston Brown's *History of the New York Stage* reports that "on the night of Dec 2 [1898], Mr. Mansfield had a nervous attack, could not go on with the performance, and the curtain was rung down and the audience dismissed." Clearly, not all actors have been able to breathe life into Rostand's gargantuan hero with equal ease.

Passionate about the play, Mansfield must nevertheless be credited with inviting Coquelin to bring the original French version to the United States. American theater circles were more than ready. Coquelin had already created a sensation in London, where the play opened on July 8, 1898, at the Lyceum Theatre. Among the special effects, real horses were brought onstage to create an equine ambience worthy of the fearless Gascon Cadets. Max Beerbohm, who at age twenty-five had just replaced George Bernard Shaw as *Saturday Review*'s drama critic, wrote a glowing account. When Coquelin finally made his American debut in December 1900, the show was immediately sold out. Rostand's French masterpiece had crossed the Atlantic and won over a new audience.

Adding to the excitement of the New York premiere and ensuring a triumphant North American tour was the casting of the most famous actress in the world at the time and perhaps the greatest diva in the history of theater: Sarah Bernhardt. Though she never acted in *Cyrano* in France, she was the only actress to interpret Roxane opposite Coquelin in the United States. Unbeknownst to many at the time, the Divine Sarah had been the original inspiration behind *Cyrano de Bergerac* and the reason Rostand wrote the role for Coquelin in the first place. She had introduced Rostand to Coquelin when the playwright came to her theater for a dramatic reading of *La Princesse lointaine*, a play he was then composing for her. Impressed by the talent of a young author who could create dramatic tension, develop stage-ready characters, and write fast-paced, poignant scenes, Coquelin told Rostand: "In my opinion, you are destined to become the greatest dramatic poet of the age. I bind myself here and now to take any play you write (in which there is a part for me) without reading it, to cancel any engagements I may have on hand, and to produce your piece with the least possible delay."* The rest is now stage history.

Enchanting as Rostand's work may be for an audience, Mansfield's case of nerves should serve as fair warning. Still today, the play represents, in the words of Kevin Kline, "treacherous waters for an actor." Kline, who starred in David Leveaux's 2007 Broadway revival of *Cyrano* at the Richard Rodgers Theatre, made his character athletic enough to engage in highly convincing feats of swordsmanship, comic enough to provoke fits of laughter, and tragic enough to inspire sympathy, if not actual pity. In a review cleverly entitled "Rapier Wit and a Nose for Poetry," Ben Brantley of the *New York Times* praised Kline's "bluster-free take on a man of bluster." Whereas Coquelin had emphasized Cyrano's bravura, and Mansfield, his sentimentality, Kline brought out his melancholy. The result was a slightly aloof version of "the hero with the long nose," a character more in keeping with a skeptical twenty-first century that calls into question age-old notions of selfless love and bravery.

Whatever fresh take revivals may bring, Cyrano will always remain such an oversized role that the success of any production hinges on that performance. Indeed, except for eleven short scenes, the lead actor never leaves the stage over the space of three hours. He must run, leap, and display extraordinary feats of swordsmanship without the slightest hint of strain or fatigue. He must switch registers at will,

* Eliot Gregory, *The Ways of Men* (Echo Library, 2005), 10.

moving seamlessly from comic to tragic to poetic to bur-
lesque mode, frequently provoking both laughter and admiration within a single scene. Thus, although the character
may seem young as written by Rostand (the real Cyrano de
Bergerac would have been twenty-one in 1640), it is nor-
mally more seasoned actors who find themselves entrusted
with the role. Witness Mansfield, at forty-one; Huster, almost
fifty; and Kline, one week shy of turning sixty. Jean-Paul Belmondo, who starred in Robert Hossein's $1.8 million pro-
duction, the hit of the 1989–90 theater season in Paris, was
fifty-six, exactly Coquelin's age when he created the role.

One supreme test, inherent to the role of all would-be
Cyranos, is having to wear a facial prosthesis large enough
to be clearly visible to the audience, yet not so voluminous
as to seem ridiculous. While born with an appendage remi-
niscent of the long-nosed *Dottore* of Italian farce, Cyrano
should never be equated with a stock figure from the *com-
media dell'arte*. He is, in fact, quite the opposite: a highly
developed character, endowed with his own unique features, both physical and moral. Nonetheless, at every performance, the theater fills with spectators come to see the
famous extremity. What, they wonder, have the props de-
partment and makeup artists done? What shape, texture,
color, and consistency will the protuberance take? Will it
be snout or beak? Broad or long? Firm or pliable? Will it
resemble Mansfield's "superstructure of putty or plaster of
Paris" so typical of the late nineteenth century, Derek Ja-
cobi's "strawberry Punchinello nose" in the Royal Shakespeare Company's 1984 production directed by Terry
Hands, or Steve Martin's Pinocchio-style protuberance in
his 1987 comic update, *Roxanne*?

Audiences are also curious to see how an actor will deliver 1,600 lines, some of them sheer poetry, with such an
obvious facial deformity. Doesn't a large prosthetic device
sitting squarely above the mouth affect the way he projects
his voice? Not if an experienced team fashions the prosthetic and a veteran actor wears it. A "proboscisly chal-
lenged" character, as Kevin Kline so aptly and humorously
describes him, Cyrano would not exist without his legendary attention-getting nose. Attaching a foreign object to his
own nose, like putting on a costume, allows the actor to get

inside the skin of his character and "find" the role. Most recently, for the 2011 adaptation of *Cyrano* at Washington's Folger Theatre, lead actor Eric Hissom and director Aaron Posner worked on finding precisely the right size and shape with Michael Meyer, an expert in makeup and special effects. They settled on a model that "pushed that edge of deformity"* and took an hour and a half to attach securely. Each evening, after the curtain dropped, the prosthetic had to be carefully removed and thrown out. A new prosthetic, with another dose of strong adhesive, was used for every performance.

Strong ticket sales at the Folger inevitably led to an extended run. In fact, performance studies show that the older Cyrano gets, the more he gains in popularity. In the past two years alone, his prominent protuberance has appeared onstage, often in multiple incarnations, in more than twenty nations, ranging from Finland to Peru. In the same time frame, there have been at least thirty different revivals and adaptations of the play just in the United States. No wonder Huster considers the role of the swashbuckling lover not only a painful "ordeal," but also the opportunity of a lifetime. Muriel Mayette, current director of the Comédie-Française, asserts she could fill all 862 seats of her illustrious theater for six months straight with a new production of *Cyrano*.

Over a century after it burst upon the world stage, *Cyrano de Bergerac* still plays to full houses, now scattered throughout the world, but today it draws different, much broader audiences. France's most popular literary figure has acquired universal appeal, spawning operas, ballets, jazz musicals, full-length movies, museum exhibits, television shows, and comic books. The reason for such fascination lies in the depth of its eponymous hero, a character who allows each of us to see some part of ourselves in him. Cyrano has become a magical mirror, able to reflect and project our pride, insecurities, egotism, and selflessness.

---

* Michele Langevine Leiby, "*Cyrano*, a Tale of Deformed Nose, Open Heart—*The Washington Post.*" *The Washington Post: National, World & D.C. Area News and Headline—The Washington Post*. Web. 17 August 2011.

Cyrano was the favorite play of President Charles de Gaulle, himself the owner, coincidentally or not, of a very large nose. Rostand's work perplexed existentialist philosopher Jean-Paul Sartre, a man acutely aware of his own unattractiveness, who struggled with the conflict between physical contingencies and spiritual exigencies. Actor Jean-Paul Belmondo, having trained early on as a professional boxer and suffered a badly broken nose in the ring, found the role irresistible. As for Gérard Depardieu, star of Jean-Paul Rappeneau's 1990 movie *Cyrano de Bergerac*, some have found him better-looking with a prosthesis, since his actual nose merits its own Facebook page.

Although Rappeneau's lavish period piece—complete with three thousand costumes and props, two thousand actors and extras, one thousand weapons, forty sets, and an entirely relandscaped forest—is the most expensive movie ever made of Rostand's classic, it was hardly the first. Paradoxically for a text so dependent on the power of words, *Cyrano* first appeared in 1925 as a silent film, directed by Augusto Genina and starring Pierre Magnier. Presented in "Pathécolor," a painstaking process of stenciling and hand-tinting each frame to highlight costumes, but sometimes also background scenes and actors' faces, it has become a classic of the genre. After receiving a Tony for his three-year run as Cyrano on Broadway, José Ferrer won the lead in Michael Gordon's low-budget black-and-white screen adaptation in 1950. His baritone voice, comedic timing, and grand gestures earned him an Academy Award and a Golden Globe, both for Best Actor. The cost of his fake nose to United Artists: $1,500. In France, Claude Dauphin (1946) and Daniel Sorano (1960) portrayed the alluring Cyrano in memorable film productions, but it is Rappeneau's opulent adaptation that has gained worldwide attention and is viewed today as the definitive cinematic version. Recipient of ten Césars (French equivalent of the Oscars), including Best Film, Actor, Cinematography, and Director, the movie also won an Oscar for Best Costume Design. For his role as the dashing but nasally challenged cadet, Depardieu was named Best Actor at the Cannes Film Festival and was even nominated for an Academy

Award as Best Actor, a remarkable accomplishment in Hollywood for a non-English-speaking role.

Fearless yet cowardly, noble yet tyrannical, clever, tongue-tied, poetic, and pathetic: no wonder movie stars and stage actors around the world feel drawn to Cyrano, for he is all of these. Mercurial in temperament while claiming to be a model of consistency, author of a dangerously deceptive game (with tragic consequences) while vaunting his own integrity, this witty swordsman is above all else a performer. As Rappeneau states in the introduction to his screenplay, "Edmond Rostand's play brings together, in a way, all the artifices of theater." For Belmondo, Cyrano does hark back to Italian farce, because he is Arlecchino *and* Pierrot, the comic figure graced with agility and the clown wearing a sad face. Careful study of the play actually shows that theatricality forms the very essence of Rostand's masterpiece, from the dazzling opening, set in the famous Théâtre de l'Hôtel de Bourgogne, to the final scene, in which the leading lady clasps her hands "in the shadowy darkness" and says with regret, "for fourteen years you played the part of an old friend" (Act Five, Scene V, page 216). In a moment of intense dramatic and situational irony, Roxane, previously blinded by what she now calls Cyrano's "imposture," sees the light just as darkness engulfs the stage and the curtain drops. Receiving the kiss that has always eluded him, Cyrano takes the ultimate final bow to an audience of one.

A consummate performer who has deluded until death the only audience he cared about, Cyrano is neither what he claims nor what he appears to be. He purports to embody freedom, yet he thrives on attention. His first act is to threaten "aggressively" and then forcibly remove the professional actor the crowd has come to watch ("Off the stage this instant, king of buffoons!" [Act One, Scene III, page 26]). The theatrical device of a play-within-a-play, dear to Rostand, Shakespeare, and so many other playwrights, does not abruptly end here, however, since Cyrano promptly replaces Montfleury's performance in Balthazar Baro's *La Clorise* with his own, in a new piece composed, directed, and acted by him, and "dramatically" entitled "Ballade of the Duel between Monsieur de Bergerac and an Imbecile, in the Hôtel de Bourgogne." Beneath the already lighted chandeliers and before an audience that includes brawlers and gamblers, bourgeois and nobles, even Cardinal Richelieu and members of the French Academy, Cyrano performs to a full house.

Charming the crowd with his impromptu scene and accomplishing a "phenomenal" and "unheard of" tour de force, the dueling poet wins over the cheering audience, as flowers and handkerchiefs rain from the balcony. In a scene that mirrors Coquelin's equally remarkable, and real-life, opening night in December 1897, the crowd swarms around its newfound hero. Like the actual cabinet minister presenting his own Legion of Honor to Coquelin, one spectator approaches Cyrano with an outstretched hand of congratulations: "It was a superb exploit. . . . It made me stamp my feet with joy!" (Act One, Scene IV, page 44). This enthusiastic admirer should know exploits when he sees them: he is none other than the famed musketeer Charles Ogier de Batz de Castelmore, Comte d'Artagnan.

To survive, an actor needs to be noticed; to thrive, he must be praised. Cyrano's personal tragedy stems from the fact that he receives recognition from everyone but praise only from those who do not count. Attention from Richelieu and d'Artagnan, Ragueneau, Le Bret, even an entire theater filled with applauding admirers may feed his ego, but not his heart. Rostand's title for Act One, "A Performance at the Hôtel de Bourgogne," thus refers both to Montfleury's botched recitation and, more important, to Cyrano's virtuoso performance, a triumph measured by the actor solely through its effect on a single spectator, Roxane. When Le Bret informs Cyrano his performance has caused her to pale, these words give him hope she might one day love him. When Roxane's duenna comes to arrange a secret meeting between the cousins, Cyrano, ever the actor (and still at the theater) falls into his confidant's arms in a particularly theatrical gesture—a swoon. Then, armed with the only response to his acting that means anything to him ("She knows I exist!"), he shouts "at the top of his lungs" for all to hear: "I need giants!" In seconds, melancholy has given way to ecstasy. An insecure braggart, who covers up his feeble self-confidence with acts of bravado, has sud-

denly become the double of Don Quixote, off on a quest to
slay giants.

Daredevil poet, Cyrano constantly thinks in terms of
theater. Often narcissistic and ostentatious, he is a man of
grandiose gestures. After shouting Montfleury off the stage
before a full house, he tosses a purse of gold coins to the
troupe he just deprived of its evening wages, in an act of
magnanimity that will leave him penniless for a month.
"What foolishness to throw it all away!" remarks Le Bret.
"Yes, but what a gesture!" replies Cyrano (Act One, Scene
IV, page 46). At the end of Act One, as he exits the stage to
fight an improbable battle against a hundred men at the
Porte de Nesle, he invites actors and actresses to follow
him, saying: "You'll add a note of Italian farce to this Spanish drama." Looking out at a picturesque moonlit cityscape,
he comments: "Ah, Paris lies before us, dim and nebulous in
the shadows, with moonlight flowing down the slopes of
her roofs! An exquisite setting for the scene about to be
performed! There, beneath the mist, the Seine quivers like
a mysterious magic mirror. . . . And you will see what you
will see!" (Act One, Scene VII, page 57).

Since Cyrano himself devises the strategy that tricks Roxane into loving Christian, many have questioned why a man
suffering from unrequited love would help a rival win his
beloved. In contriving his scheme, which Christian calls
frightening and later insists on abandoning, Cyrano writes
the one scenario that lets him play the part of the lover.
Burdened by the all-consuming conviction that Roxane
will never see beyond his "poor monstrous nose" ("I have
no illusions" [Act One, Scene V, page 50]), he enters into a
Faustian bargain with the handsome young cadet, an "experiment" by which they become one. Cyrano allows his
soul to pass into his rival's body in exchange for the right to
play his dream role. The ideal Romantic hero they form to
woo Roxane proves a less than admirable creation, however, since it leads to Christian's death, traps Cyrano in a
lie, and condemns Roxane to a lifetime of mourning. Ironically, in this love triangle, the ugly but chivalrous poet, who
composes florid declarations of love and boasts of his integrity, rejects Christian's suggestion that they break the
pact and grant Roxane the right to choose whom she loves.

Cyrano insists his "moral grooming is impeccable": he never appears in public "with a soiled conscience," always holds "[his] soul erect," making "truths ring like spurs" (Act One, Scene IV, page 40). Yet it is Christian, the one who never boasts of his honesty, who ultimately does what is right. Unlike his partner in deception, he chooses to abandon the life of an actor: "I'm tired . . . of always playing a part!" (Act Three, Scene IV, page 118).

At the beginning of the play, when Le Bret asks his friend what he is trying to accomplish with his life, Cyrano brashly explains that he was once bewildered by the many courses of action open to him and then chose to limit himself to a single option: "I decided to be admirable in everything!" (Act One, Scene V, page 48). Admirable or not, Edmond Rostand's most famous protagonist has for the past hundred years acted like a magnet for stage and screen actors, makeup artists, singers, scholars, and students of literature and performance studies. Ever since he took Paris by storm on December 28, 1897, a day that will remain a milestone in the history of theater, he has attracted uncommon attention and provoked spirited debate. Constant Coquelin, José Ferrer, Kevin Kline, and Gérard Depardieu stand as but a few among scores of exceptional actors who, across generations, have left their indelible mark on the astonishingly complex, many-layered character Francis Huster once called, quite simply and enigmatically, the hero with the long nose.

—Cynthia B. Kerr

Selected Bibliography

PLAYS BY EDMOND ROSTAND

Le gant rouge (The Red Glove) (With Henry Lee) 1888

Les romanesque (The Romancers) 1894

La princesse lointaine (The Far Princess) 1895

La Samaritaine (The Woman of Samaria) 1897

Cyrano de Bergerac 1897

L'Aiglon (The Eaglet) 1900

Chantecler (1910)

La dernière nuit de don Juan (The Last Night of Don Juan) 1922

BIOGRAPHY AND CRITICISM

Amoia, Alba della Fazia. *Edmond Rostand*. Boston: Twayne, 1978.

Chweh, Crystal R., ed. *Readings on* Cyrano de Bergerac. San Diego: Greenhaven Press, 2001.

Freeman, E. J. *Edmond Rostand,* Cyrano de Bergerac. Glasgow: University of Glasgow French and German Publications, 1995.

Harth, Erica. Cyrano de Bergerac *and the Polemics of Modernity*. New York: Columbia University Press, 1970.

Lanius, Edward W. Cyrano de Bergerac *and the Universe of Imagination*. Geneva: Droz, 1967.

Rostand, Edmond. *Cyrano de Bergerac.* Geoff Woollen. ed. London: Bristol Classical Press, 1994.

Connect with Berkley Publishing Online!

For sneak peeks into the newest releases, news on all your favorite authors, book giveaways, and a central place to connect with fellow fans—

"Like" and follow Berkley Publishing!

facebook.com/BerkleyPub
twitter.com/BerkleyPub
instagram.com/BerkleyPub

Penguin
Random
House